the **killer**
inside me

Other titles available in Vintage Crime/Black Lizard

by Jim Thompson

After Dark, My Sweet
The Getaway
The Grifters
A Hell of a Woman
Nothing More Than Murder

by Charles Willeford

The Burnt Orange Heresy
Cockfighter
Pick-Up

by David Goodis

Black Friday
The Burglar
Nightfall
Shoot the Piano Player
Street of No Return

by Charles Williams

The Hot Spot

by Fredric Brown

The Far Cry
His Name Was Death

by Richard Neely

The Plastic Nightmare

the **killer inside me**

jim thompson

VINTAGE CRIME / **BLACK LIZARD**

vintage books • a division of random house, inc. • new york

First Vintage Crime/Black Lizard Edition, March 1991

Library of Congress Cataloging-in-Publication Data
Thompson, Jim, 1906–1977.
The killer inside me / Jim Thompson.
p.   cm.—(Vintage crime/Black Lizard)
ISBN 0-679-73397-3
I. Title.   II. Series: Vintage crime/Black Lizard.
PS3539.H6733K5   1991
813′.54—dc20   90-50472 CIP

Manufactured in the United States of America
10 9 8 7 6 5 4 3 2 1

the **killer
inside me**

1

I'd finished my pie and was having a second cup of coffee when I saw him. The midnight freight had come in a few minutes before; and he was peering in one end of the restaurant window, the end nearest the depot, shading his eyes with his hand and blinking against the light. He saw me watching him, and his face faded back into the shadows. But I knew he was still there. I knew he was waiting. The bums always size me up for an easy mark.

I lit a cigar and slid off my stool. The waitress, a new girl from Dallas, watched as I buttoned my coat. "Why, you don't even carry a gun!" she said, as though she was giving me a piece of news.

"No," I smiled. "No gun, no blackjack, nothing like that. Why should I?"

"But you're a cop—a deputy sheriff, I mean. What if some crook should try to shoot you?"

"We don't have many crooks here in Central City, ma'am," I said. "Anyway, people are people, even when they're a little misguided. You don't hurt them, they won't hurt you. They'll listen to reason."

She shook her head, wide-eyed with awe, and I strolled up to the front. The proprietor shoved back my money and laid a couple of cigars on top of it. He thanked me again for taking his son in hand.

"He's a different boy now, Lou," he said, kind of running his words together like foreigners do. "Stays in nights; gets along fine in school. And always he talks about you—what a good man is Deputy Lou Ford."

"I didn't do anything," I said. "Just talked to him. Showed him a little interest. Anyone else could have done as much."

"Only you," he said. "Because you are good, you make others so." He was all ready to sign off with that, but I wasn't. I leaned an elbow on the counter, crossed one foot behind the other and took a long slow drag on my cigar. I liked the guy—as much as I like most people, anyway—but he was too good to let go. Polite, intelligent: guys like that are my meat.

"Well, I tell you," I drawled. "I tell you the way I look at it, a man doesn't get any more out of life than what he puts into it."

"Umm," he said, fidgeting. "I guess you're right, Lou."

"I was thinking the other day, Max; and all of a sudden I had the doggonedest thought. It came to me out of a clear sky—the boy is father to the man. Just like that. The boy is father to the man."

The smile on his face was getting strained. I could hear his shoes creak as he squirmed. If there's anything worse than a bore, it's a corny bore. But how can you brush off a nice friendly fellow who'd give you his shirt if you asked for it?

"I reckon I should have been a college professor or something like that," I said. "Even when I'm asleep I'm working out problems. Take that heat wave we had a few weeks ago; a lot of people think it's the heat that makes it so hot. But it's not like that, Max. It's not the heat, but the humidity. I'll bet you didn't know that, did you?"

He cleared his throat and muttered something about being wanted in the kitchen. I pretended like I didn't hear him.

"Another thing about the weather," I said. "Everyone talks about it, but no one does anything. But maybe it's better that way. Every cloud has its silver lining, at least that's the way I figure it. I mean, if we didn't have the rain we wouldn't have the rainbows, now would we?"

"Lou . . ."

"Well," I said, "I guess I'd better shove off. I've got quite a bit of getting around to do, and I don't want to rush. Haste makes waste, in my opinion. I like to look before I leap."

That was dragging 'em in by the feet, but I couldn't hold 'em back. Striking at people that way is almost as good as the other, the real way. The way I'd fought to forget—and had almost forgot—until I met her.

I was thinking about her as I stepped out into the cool West Texas night and saw the bum waiting for me.

2

Central City was founded in 1870, but it never became a city in size until about ten-twelve years ago. It was a shipping point for a lot of cattle and a little cotton; and Chester Conway, who was born here, made it headquarters for the Conway Construction Company. But it still wasn't much more than a wide place in a Texas road. Then, the oil boom came, and almost overnight the population jumped to 48,000.

Well, the town had been laid out in a little valley amongst a lot of hills. There just wasn't any room for the newcomers, so they spread out every whichway with their homes and businesses, and now they were scattered across a third of the county. It's not an unusual situation in the oil-boom country—you'll see a lot of cities like ours if you're ever out this way. They don't have any regular city police force, just a constable or two. The sheriff's office handles the policing for both city and county.

We do a pretty good job of it, to our own way of thinking at least. But now and then things get a little out of hand, and we put on a cleanup. It was during a cleanup three months ago that I ran into her.

"Name of Joyce Lakeland," old Bob Maples, the sheriff, told me. "Lives four-five miles out on Derrick Road, just past the old Branch farm house. Got her a nice little cottage up there behind a stand of blackjack trees."

"I think I know the place," I said. "Hustlin' lady, Bob?"

"We-el, I reckon so but she's bein' mighty decent about it. She ain't running it into the ground, and she ain't takin' on no roustabouts or sheepherders. If some of these preachers around town wasn't rompin' on me, I wouldn't bother her a-tall."

I wondered if he was getting some of it, and decided that he wasn't. He wasn't maybe any mental genius, but Bob Maples was straight. "So how shall I handle this Joyce Lakeland?" I said. "Tell her to lay off a while, or to move on?"

"We-el," he scratched his head, scowling—"I dunno, Lou. Just—well, just go out and size her up, and make your own decision. I know you'll be gentle, as gentle and pleasant as you can be. An' I know you can be firm if you have to. So go on out, an' see how she looks to you. I'll back you up in whatever you want to do."

It was about ten o'clock in the morning when I got there. I pulled the car up into the yard, curving it around so I could swing out easy. The county license plates didn't show, but it wasn't deliberate. It was just the way it had to be.

I eased up on the porch, knocked on the door and stood back, taking off my Stetson.

I was feeling a little uncomfortable. I hardly knew what I was going to say to her. Because maybe we're kind of old-fashioned, but our standards of conduct aren't the same, say, as they are in the east or middle-west. Out here you say yes ma'am and no ma'am to anything with skirts on; anything white, that is. Out here, if you catch a man with his pants down, you apologize . . . even if you have to arrest him afterwards. Out here you're a man, a man and a gentleman, or you aren't anything. And God help you if you're not.

The door opened an inch or two. Then, it opened all the way and she stood looking at me.

"Yes?" she said coldly.

She was wearing sleeping shorts and a wool pullover; her brown hair was as tousled as a lamb's tail, and her unpainted face was drawn with sleep. But none of that mattered. It wouldn't have mattered if she'd crawled out of a hog-wallow wearing a gunny sack. She had that much.

She yawned openly and said "Yes?" again, but I still couldn't speak. I guess I was staring open-mouthed like a country boy. This was three months ago, remember, and I hadn't had the sickness in almost fifteen years. Not since I was fourteen.

She wasn't much over five feet and a hundred pounds, and she looked a little scrawny around the neck and ankles. But that was all right. It was perfectly all right. The good Lord had known just where to put that flesh where it would *really* do some good.

"Oh, my goodness!" She laughed suddenly. "Come on in. I don't make a practice of it this early in the morning, but . . ." She held the screen open and gestured. I went in and she closed it and locked the door again.

"I'm sorry, ma'am," I said, "but—"

"It's all right. But I'll have to have some coffee first. You go on back."

I went down the little hall to the bedroom, listening uneasily as I heard her drawing water for the coffee. I'd acted like a chump. It was going to be hard to be firm with her after a start like this, and something told me I should be. I didn't know why; I still don't. But I knew it right from the beginning. Here was a little lady who got what she wanted, and to hell with the price tag.

Well, hell, though; it was just a feeling. She'd acted all right, and she had a nice quiet little place here. I decided I'd let her ride, for the time being anyhow. Why not? And then I happened to glance into the dresser mirror and I knew why not. I knew I couldn't. The top dresser drawer was open a little, and the mirror was tilted slightly. And hustling ladies are one thing, and hustling ladies with guns are something else.

I took it out of the drawer, a .32 automatic, just as she came in with the coffee tray. Her eyes flashed and she slammed the tray down on a table. "What," she snapped, "are you doing with that?"

I opened my coat and showed her my badge. "Sheriff's office, ma'am. What are *you* doing with it?"

She didn't say anything. She just took her purse off the dresser, opened it and pulled out a permit. It had been issued in Fort Worth, but it was all legal enough. Those things are usually honored from one town to another.

"Satisfied, copper?" she said.

"I reckon it's all right, miss," I said. "And my name's Ford, not copper." I gave her a big smile, but I didn't get any back. My hunch about her had been dead right. A minute before she'd been all set to lay, and it probably wouldn't have made any difference if I hadn't had a dime. Now she was set for something else, and whether I was a cop or Christ didn't make any difference either.

I wondered how she'd lived so long.

"Jesus!" she jeered. "The nicest looking guy I ever saw and you turn out to be a lousy snooping copper. How much? I don't jazz cops."

I felt my face turning red. "Lady," I said, "that's not very polite. I just came out for a little talk."

"You dumb bastard," she yelled. "I asked you what you wanted."

"Since you put it that way," I said, "I'll tell you. I want you out of Central City by sundown. If I catch you here after that I'll run you in for prostitution."

I slammed on my hat and started for the door. She got in front of me, blocking the way.

"You lousy son-of-a-bitch. You—"

"Don't you call me that," I said. "Don't do it, ma'am."

"I did call you that! And I'll do it again! You're a son-of-a-bitch, bastard, pimp. . . ."

I tried to push past her. I had to get out of there. I knew what was going to happen if I didn't get out, and I knew I couldn't let it happen. I might kill her. It might bring *the sickness* back. And even if I didn't and it didn't, I'd be washed up. She'd talk. She'd yell her head off. And people would start thinking, thinking and wondering about that time fifteen years ago.

She slapped me so hard that my ears rang, first on one side then the other. She swung and kept swinging. My hat flew off. I stooped to pick it up, and she slammed her knee under my chin.

I stumbled backward on my heels and sat down on the floor. I heard a mean laugh, then another laugh sort of apologetic. She said, "Gosh, sheriff, I didn't mean to—I—you made me so mad I—I—"

"Sure," I grinned. My vision was clearing and I found my voice again. "Sure, ma'am, I know how it was. Used to get that way myself. Give me a hand, will you?"

"You-you won't hurt me?"

"Me? Aw, now, ma'am."

"No," she said, and she sounded almost disappointed. "I know you won't. Anyone can see you're too easy-going." And she came over to me slowly and gave me her hands.

I pulled myself up. I held her wrists with one hand and swung. It almost stunned her; I didn't want her completely stunned. I wanted her so she would understand what was happening to her.

"No, baby"—my lips drew back from my teeth. "I'm not going to hurt you. I wouldn't think of hurting you. I'm just going to beat the ass plumb off of you."

I said it, and I meant it and I damned near did.

I jerked the jersey up over her face and tied the end in a knot. I threw her down on the bed, yanked off her sleeping shorts and tied her feet together with them.

I took off my belt and raised it over my head. . . .

I don't know how long it was before I stopped, before I came to my senses. All I know is that my arm ached like hell and her rear end was one big bruise, and I was scared crazy—as scared as a man can get and go on living.

I freed her feet and hands, and pulled the jersey off her head. I soaked a towel in cold water and bathed her with it. I poured coffee between her lips. And all the time I was talking, begging her to forgive me, telling her how sorry I was.

I got down on my knees by the bed, and begged and apologized. At last her eyelids fluttered and opened.

"D-don't," she whispered.

"I won't," I said. "Honest to God, ma'am, I won't ever—"

"Don't talk." She brushed her lips against mine. "Don't say you're sorry."

She kissed me again. She began fumbling at my tie, my

shirt; starting to undress me after I'd almost skinned her alive.

I went back the next day and the day after that. I kept going back. And it was like a wind had been turned on a dying fire. I began needling people in that dead-pan way—needling 'em as a substitute for something else. I began thinking about settling scores with Chester Conway, of the Conway Construction Company.

I won't say that I hadn't thought of it before. Maybe I'd stayed on in Central City all these years, just in the hopes of getting even. But except for her I don't think I'd ever have done anything. She'd made the old fire burn again. She even showed me how to square with Conway.

She didn't know she was doing it, but she gave me the answer. It was one day, one night rather, about six weeks after we'd met.

"Lou," she said, "I don't want to go on like this. Let's pull out of this crummy town together, just you and I."

"Why, you're crazy!" I said. I said it before I could stop myself. "You think I'd—I'd—"

"Go on, Lou. Let me hear you say it. Tell me"—she began to drawl—"what a fine ol' family you-all Fords is. Tell me, we-all Fords, ma'am, we wouldn't think of livin' with one of you mizzable ol' whores, ma'am. Us Fords just ain't built that way, ma'am."

That was part of it, a big part. But it wasn't the main thing. I knew she was making me worse; I knew that if I didn't stop soon I'd never be able to. I'd wind up in a cage or the electric chair.

"Say it, Lou. Say it and I'll say something."

"Don't threaten me, baby," I said. "I don't like threats."

"I'm not threatening you. I'm telling you. You think you're too good for me—I'll—I'll—"

"Go on. It's your turn to do the saying."

"I wouldn't want to, Lou, honey, but I'm not going to give you up. Never, never, never. If you're too good for me now, then I'll make it so you won't be."

I kissed her, a long hard kiss. Because baby didn't know it, but baby was dead, and in a way I couldn't have loved her more.

"Well, now, baby," I said, "you've got your bowels in an uproar and all over nothing. I was thinking about the money problem."

"I've got some money. I can get some more. A lot of it."

"Yeah?"

"I can, Lou. I know I can! He's crazy about me and he's dumb as hell. I'll bet if his old man thought I was going to marry him, he—"

"Who?" I said. "Who are you talking about, Joyce?"

"Elmer Conway. You know who he is, don't you? Old Chester—"

"Yeah," I said. "Yeah, I know the Conways right well. How do you figure on hookin' 'em?"

We talked it over, lying there on her bed together, and off in the night somewhere a voice seemed to whisper to forget it, *forget it, Lou, it's not too late if you stop now.* And I did try, God knows I tried. But right after that, right after the voice, her hand gripped one of mine and

kneaded it into her breasts; and she moaned and shivered
. . . and so I didn't forget.

"Well," I said, after a time, "I guess we can work it out.
The way I see it is, if at first you don't succeed, try, try
again."

"Mmm, darling?"

"In other words," I said, "where there's a will there's a
way."

She squirmed a little, and then she snickered. "Oh, Lou,
you corny so and so! You slay me!"

. . . The street was dark. I was standing a few doors above
the cafe, and the bum was standing and looking at me.
He was a young fellow, about my age, and he was wearing what must have been a pretty good suit of clothes at
one time.

"Well, how about it, bud?" he was saying. "How about
it, huh? I've been on a hell of a binge, and by God if I
don't get some food pretty soon—"

"Something to warm you up, eh?" I said.

"Yeah, anything at all you can help me with, I'll . . ."

I took the cigar out of my mouth with one hand and
made like I was reaching into my pocket with the other.
Then, I grabbed his wrist and ground the cigar butt into
his palm.

"Jesus, bud!"—he cursed and jerked away from me.
"What the hell you tryin' to do?"

I laughed and let him see my badge. "Beat it," I said.

"Sure, bud, sure," he said, and he began backing away.

He didn't sound particularly scared or angry; more interested than anything. "But you better watch that stuff, bud. You sure better watch it."

He turned and walked off toward the railroad tracks.

I watched him, feeling sort of sick and shaky; and then I got in my car and headed for the labor temple.

3

The Central City Labor Temple was on a side street a couple of blocks off of the courthouse square. It wasn't much of a building, an old two-story brick with the downstairs rented out to a pool hall and the union offices and meeting hall on the second floor. I climbed the stairs, and went down the dark corridor to the end where a door opened into several of the best and largest offices in the place. The sign on the glass read

CENTRAL CITY, TEXAS
Building Trades Council
Joseph Rothman, Pres.

and Rothman opened the door before I could turn the knob.

"Let's go back here in the rear," he said, shaking hands. "Sorry to ask you to come around so late, but with you being a public official and all I thought it might be best."

"Yeah," I nodded, wishing I could have ducked seeing

him entirely. The law is pretty much on one side of the fence out here; and I already knew what he wanted to talk about.

He was a man of about forty, short and stocky, with sharp black eyes and a head that seemed too big for his body. He had a cigar in his mouth, but he laid it down after he sat down at his desk, and began rolling a cigarette. He lit it and blew smoke over the match, his eyes shying away from mine.

"Lou," the labor leader said, and hesitated. "I've got something to tell you—in the strictest confidence, you understand—but I'd like you to tell me something first. It's probably a pretty touchy subject with you, but . . . well, how did you feel about Mike Dean, Lou?"

"Feel? I'm not sure I know what you mean, Joe," I said.

"He was your foster brother, right? Your father adopted him?"

"Yes. Dad was a doctor, you know—"

"And a very good one, I understand. Excuse me, Lou. Go on."

So that's the way it was going to be. Spar and counter-spar. Each of us feeling the other out, each of us telling things he knows damn well the other fellow has heard a thousand times. Rothman had something important to tell me, and it looked as though he was going to do it the hard—and careful—way. Well, I didn't mind; I'd play along with him.

"He and the Deans were old friends. When they got wiped out in that big flu epidemic, he adopted Mike. My mother was dead—had been dead since I was a baby. Dad figured Mike and me would be company for each other, and the housekeeper could take care of two of us as easily as one."

"Uh-huh. And how did that strike you, Lou? I mean, you're the only son and heir and your dad brings in another son. Didn't that rub you a little the wrong way?"

I laughed. "Hell, Joe, I was four years old at the time, and Mike was six. You're not much concerned with money at that age, and, anyway, Dad never had any. He was too softhearted to dun his patients."

"You liked Mike, then?" He sounded like he wasn't quite convinced.

"Like isn't the word for it," I said. "He was the finest, swellest guy that ever lived. I couldn't have loved a real brother more."

"Even after he did what he did?"

"And just what," I drawled, "would that be?"

Rothman raised his eyebrows. "I liked Mike myself, Lou, but facts are facts. The whole town knows that if he'd been a little older he'd have gone to the chair instead of reform school."

"No one *knows* anything. There was never any proof."

"The girl identified him."

"A girl less than three years old! She'd have identified anyone they showed her."

"And Mike admitted it. And they dug up some other cases."

"Mike was scared. He didn't know what he was saying."

Rothman shook his head. "Let it go, Lou. I'm not really interested in that as such; only in your feelings about Mike. . . . Weren't you pretty embarrassed when he came back to Central City? Wouldn't it have been better if he'd stayed away?"

"No," I said. "Dad and I knew Mike hadn't done it. I mean"—I hesitated—"knowing Mike, we were sure he couldn't be guilty." *Because I was. Mike had taken the blame for me.* "I wanted Mike to come back. So did Dad." *He wanted him here to watch over me.* "My God, Joe, Dad pulled strings for months to get Mike his job as city building inspector. It wasn't easy to do, the way people felt about Mike, as popular and influential as Dad was."

"That all checks," Rothman nodded. "That's my understanding of things. But I have to be sure. You weren't sort of relieved when Mike got killed?"

"The shock killed Dad. He never recovered from it. As for me, well all I can say is that I wish it had been me instead of Mike."

Rothman grinned. "Okay, Lou. Now it's my turn. . . . Mike was killed six years ago. He was walking a girder on the eighth floor of the New Texas Apartments, a Conway Construction job, when he apparently stepped on a loose rivet. He threw himself backward so he'd fall inside the building, onto the decking. But the floors hadn't been decked in properly; there were just a few planks scattered here and there. Mike fell all the way through to the basement."

I nodded. "So," I said. "What about it, Joe?"

"What about it!" Rothman's eyes flashed. "You ask me what about it when—"

"As President of the building unions, you know that the Ironworkers are under your jurisdiction, Joe. It's their obligation, and yours, to see that each floor is decked in as a building goes up."

"Now you're talking like a lawyer!" Rothman slapped his desk. "The Ironworkers are weak out here. Conway wouldn't put in the decking, and we couldn't make him."

"You could have struck the job."

"Oh, well," Rothman shrugged. "I guess I made a mistake, Lou. I understood you to say that you—"

"You heard me right," I said. "And let's not kid each other. Conway cut corners to make money. You let him— to make money. I'm not saying you're at fault, but I don't reckon he was either. It was just one of those things."

"Well," Rothman hesitated, "that's a kind of funny attitude for you to take, Lou. It seems to me you're pretty impersonal about it. But since that's the way you feel, perhaps I'd better—"

"Perhaps *I'd* better," I said. "Let me do the talking and then you won't have to feel funny about it. There was a riveter up there with Mike at the time he took his dive. Working after hours. Working by himself. But it takes two men to rivet—one to run the gun and one on the bucking iron. You're going to tell me that he didn't have any rightful business there, but I think you're wrong. He didn't have to be riveting. He could have been gathering up tools or something like that."

"But you don't know the whole story, Lou! This man—"

"I know. The guy was an iron tramp, working on a permit. He blew into town without a dime. Three days after Mike's death he left in a new Chevy which he paid cash on the line for. That looks bad, but it doesn't really need to mean anything. He might have won the dough in a crap game or—"

"But you still don't know it all, Lou! Conway—"

"Let's see if I don't," I said. "Conway's company was the architect on that job as well as the contractor. And he hadn't allowed enough space for the boilers. To get 'em in, he was going to have to make certain alterations which he knew damned well Mike would never allow. It was either that or lose several hundred thousand dollars."

"Go on, Lou."

"So he took the loss. He hated it like hell, but he went ahead and did it."

Rothman laughed shortly. "He did, huh? I pushed iron on that job, myself, and—and—"

"Well." I gave him a puzzled look. "He did, didn't he? No matter what happened to Mike, your locals couldn't close their eyes to a dangerous situation like that. You're responsible. You can be sued. You could be tried for criminal collusion. You—"

"Lou." Rothman cleared his throat. "You're a hundred per cent right, Lou. Naturally we wouldn't stick our necks out for any amount of money."

"Sure," I smiled stupidly. "You just haven't thought this deal through, Joe. You've been getting along pretty good with Conway, and now he's taken a notion to go non-union, and naturally you're kind of upset about it. I reckon if you thought there'd really been a murder you wouldn't have waited six years to speak up."

"Yeah, I mean certainly not. Certainly, I wouldn't." He began rolling another cigarette. "Uh, how did you find out all these things, Lou, if you don't mind telling me?"

"Well, you know how it is. Mike was a member of the family, and I get around a lot. Any talk that's going around, I'd naturally hear it."

"Mmmm. I didn't realize there'd been so much gossip. In fact, I didn't know there'd been any. And you never felt inclined to take any action?"

"Why should I?" I said. "It was just gossip. Conway's a big business man—just about the biggest contractor in West Texas. He wouldn't get mixed up in a murder any more'n you people would keep quiet about one."

Rothman gave me another sharp look, and then he looked down at his desk. "Lou," he said softly, "do you know how many days a year an ironworker works? Do you know what his life expectancy is? Did you ever see an old ironworker? Did you ever stop to figure that there's all kinds of ways of dying, but only one way of being dead?"

"Well, no. I reckon not," I said. "I guess I don't know what you're driving at, Joe."

"Let it go. It's not really relevant."

"I suppose the boys don't have it too easy," I said. "But here's the way I look at it, Joe. There's no law says they have to stick to one line of work. If they don't like it they can do something else."

"Yeah," he nodded, "that's right, isn't it? It's funny how it takes an outsider to see through these problems. . . . If they don't like it let 'em do something else. That's good, that's very good."

"Aw," I said, "it wasn't anything much."

"I disagree. It's very enlightening. You really surprise me, Lou. I've been seeing you around town for years and frankly you hardly struck me as a deep thinker. . . . Do you have any solution for our larger problems, the Negro situation for example?"

"Well, that's pretty simple," I said. "I'd just ship 'em all to Africa."

"Uh-huh. I see, I see," he said, and he stood up and held out his hand. "I'm sorry I troubled you for nothing, Lou, but I've certainly enjoyed our talk. I hope we can get together again sometime."

"That would be nice," I said.

"Meanwhile, of course, I haven't seen you. Understand?"

"Oh, sure," I said.

We talked for a minute or two more, and then we walked to the outside door together. He glanced at it sharply, then looked at me. "Say," he said. "Didn't I close that damned thing?"

"I thought you did," I said.

"Well, no harm done, I guess," he said. "Could I make a suggestion to you, Lou, in your own interests?"

"Why, sure you can, Joe. Anything at all."

"Save that bullshit for the birds."

He nodded, grinning at me; and for a minute you could have heard a pin drop. But he wasn't going to say anything. He wasn't ever going to let on. So, finally, I began to grin, too.

"I don't know the why of it, Lou—I don't know a thing, understand? Not a thing. But watch yourself. It's a good act but it's easy to overdo."

"You kind of asked for it, Joe," I said.

"And now you know why. And I'm not very bright or I wouldn't be a labor skate."

"Yeah," I said. "I see what you mean."

We shook hands again and he winked and bobbed his head. And I went down the dark hall and down the stairs.

4

After Dad died I'd thought about selling our house. I'd had several good offers for it, in fact, since it was right on the edge of the downtown business district; but somehow I couldn't let it go. The taxes were pretty high and there was ten times as much room as I needed, but I couldn't bring myself to sell. Something told me to hold on, to wait.

I drove down the alley to our garage. I drove in and shut off the lights. The garage had been a barn; it still was, for that matter; and I sat there in the doorway, sniffing the musty odors of old oats and hay and straw, dreaming back through the years. Mike and I had kept our ponies in those two front stalls, and back here in the box stall we'd had an outlaws' cave. We'd hung swings and acting bars from these rafters; and we'd made a swimming pool out of the horse trough. And up overhead in the loft, where the rats now scampered and scurried, Mike had found me with the little gi—

A rat screamed suddenly on a high note.

I got out of the car and hurried out of the big sliding

door of the barn, and into the backyard. I wondered if that was why I stayed here: To punish myself.

I went in the back door of the house and went through the house to the front, turning on all the lights, the downstairs lights I mean. Then I came back into the kitchen and made coffee and carried the pot up into Dad's old office. I sat in his big old leather chair, sipping coffee and smoking, and gradually the tension began to leave me.

It had always made me feel better to come here, back from the time I was kneehigh to a grasshopper. It was like coming out of the darkness into sunlight, out of a storm into calm. Like being lost and found again.

I got up and walked along the bookcases, and endless files of psychiatric literature, the bulky volumes of morbid psychology . . . Krafft-Ebing, Jung, Freud, Bleuler, Adolf Meyer, Kretschmer, Kraepelin. . . . All the answers were here, out in the open where you could look at them. And no one was terrified or horrified. I came out of the place I was hiding in—that I always had to hide in—and began to breathe.

I took down a bound volume of one of the German periodicals and read a while. I put it back and took down one in French. I skimmed through an article in Spanish and another in Italian. I couldn't speak any of those languages worth a doggone, but I could understand 'em all. I'd just picked 'em up with Dad's help, just like I'd picked up some higher mathematics and physical chemistry and half a dozen other subjects.

Dad had wanted me to be a doctor, but he was afraid to have me go away to school so he'd done what he could for me at home. It used to irritate him, knowing what I had in my head, to hear me talking and acting like any other rube around town. But, in time, when he realized how bad I had *the sickness*, he even encouraged me to do it. That's what I was going to be; I was going to have to live and get along with rubes. I wasn't ever going to have anything but some safe, small job, and I'd have to act accordingly. If Dad could have swung anything else that paid a living, I wouldn't even have been as much as a deputy sheriff.

I fiddled around Dad's desk, working out a couple of problems in calculus just for the hell of it. Turning away from the desk, I looked at myself in the mirrored door of the laboratory.

I was still wearing my Stetson, shoved a little to the back of my head. I had on a kind of pinkish shirt and a black bow tie, and the pants of my blue serge suit were hitched up so as to catch on the tops of my Justin boots. Lean and wiry; a mouth that looked all set to drawl. A typical Western-country peace officer, that was me. Maybe friendlier looking than the average. Maybe a little cleaner cut. But on the whole typical.

That's what I was, and I couldn't change. Even if it was safe, I doubted if I could change. I'd pretended so long that I no longer had to.

"Lou . . ."

I jumped and whirled.

"Amy!" I gasped. "What in the—You shouldn't be here! Where—"

"Upstairs, waiting for you. Now, don't get excited,

Lou. I slipped out after the folks went to sleep and you know them."

"But someone might—"

"No one did. I slipped down the alley. Aren't you glad?"

I wasn't, although I suppose I should have been. She didn't have the shape that Joyce did, but it was a big improvement over anything else around Central City. Except when she stuck her chin out and narrowed her eyes, like she was daring you to cross her, she was a mighty pretty girl.

"Well, sure," I said. "Sure, I'm glad. Let's go back up, huh?"

I followed her up the stairs and into my bedroom. She kicked off her shoes, tossed her coat on a chair with her other clothes, and flopped down backwards on the bed.

"My!" she said, after a moment; and her chin began to edge outward. "Such enthusiasm!"

"Oh," I said, giving my head a shake. "I'm sorry, Amy. I had something on my mind."

"S-something on your mind!" Her voice quavered. "I strip myself for him, I shed my decency and my clothes for him and h-he stands there with 'something' on his m-mind!"

"Aw, now, honey. It's just that I wasn't expecting you, and—"

"No! And why should you? The way you avoid me and make excuses for not seeing me. If I had any pride left I'd—I'd—"

She buried her head in the pillow and began to sob, giving me an A-1 view of what was probably the second prettiest rear end in West Texas. I was pretty sure she was faking; I'd picked up a lot of pointers on women from Joyce. But I didn't dare give her the smacking she deserved. Instead I threw off my own clothes and crawled into bed with her, pulling her around facing me.

"Now, cut it out, honey," I said. "You know I've just been busy as a chigger at a picnic."

"I don't know it! I don't know anything of the kind! You don't want to be with me, that's what!"

"Why, that's plumb crazy, honey. Why wouldn't I want to?"

"B-because. Oh, Lou, darling, I've been so miserable. . . ."

"Well, now that's a right foolish way to act, Amy," I said.

She went on whimpering about how miserable she'd been, and I went on holding her, listening—you got to do plenty of listening around Amy—and wondering how it had all started.

To tell the truth, I guess it hadn't started anywhere. We'd just drifted together like straws in a puddle. Our families had grown up together, and we'd grown up together, right here in this same block. We'd walked back and forth to school together, and when we went to parties we were paired off together. We hadn't needed to do anything. It was all done for us.

I suppose half the town, including her own folks, knew we were knocking off a little. But no one said anything or thought anything about it. After all we were going to get married . . . even if we were kind of taking our time.

"Lou!" she nudged me. "You aren't listening to me!"

"Why, sure, I am, honey."

"Well, answer me then."

"Not now," I said. "I've got something else on my mind, now."

"But . . . Oh, *darling* . . ."

I figured she'd been gabbing and nagging about nothing, as usual, and she'd forget about whatever I was supposed to answer. But it didn't work out that way. As soon as it was over and I'd reached her cigarettes for her, taking one for myself, she gave me another one of her looks and another, "Well, Lou?"

"I hardly know what to say," I said, which was exactly the case.

"You want to marry me, don't you?"

"Mar—but, sure," I said.

"I think we've waited long enough, Lou. I can go on teaching school. We'll get by a lot better than most couples."

"But . . . but that's all we'd do, Amy. We'd never get anywhere!"

"What do you mean?"

"Well, I don't want to go on being a deputy sheriff all of my life. I want to—well—be somebody."

"Like what, for example?"

"Oh, I don't know. There's no use in talking about it."

"A doctor, perhaps? I think that would be awfully nice. Is that what you had in mind, Lou?"

"I know it's crazy, Amy. But—"

She laughed. She rolled her head on the pillow, laughing. "Oh, Lou! I never heard of such a thing! You're twenty-nine years old, and y-you don't even speak good English, and—and—oh, ha, ha, ha . . ."

She laughed until she was gasping, and my cigarette burned down between my fingers and I never knew it until I smelled the scorching flesh.

"I'm s-sorry, darling. I didn't mean to hurt your feelings, but—Were you teasing me? Were you joking with your little Amy?"

"You know me," I said. "Lou the laughing boy."

She began to quiet down at the tone of my voice. She turned away from me and lay on her back, picking at the quilt with her fingers. I got up and found a cigar, and sat down on the bed again.

"You don't want to marry me, do you, Lou?"

"I don't think we should marry now, no."

"You don't want to marry me at all."

"I didn't say that."

She was silent for several minutes, but her face talked for her. I saw her eyes narrow and a mean little smile twist her lips, and I knew what she was thinking. I knew almost to a word what she was going to say.

"I'm afraid you'll have to marry me, Lou. You'll have to, do you understand?"

"No," I said. "I won't have to. You're not pregnant, Amy. You've never gone with anyone else, and you're not pregnant by me."

"I'm lying, I suppose?"

"Seems as though," I said. "I couldn't get you pregnant if I wanted to. I'm sterile."

"*You?*"

"Sterile isn't the same thing as impotent. I've had a vasectomy."

"Then why have we always been so—why do you use—?"

I shrugged. "It saved a lot of explanations. Anyway, you're not pregnant, to get back to the subject."

"I just don't understand," she said, frowning. She wasn't at all bothered by my catching her in a lie. "Your father did it? Why, Lou?"

"Oh, I was kind of run down and nervous, and he thought—"

"Why, you were not! You were never that way!"

"Well," I said, "he thought I was."

"He *thought!* He did a terrible thing like that—made you so we can never have children—just because he thought something! Why, it's terrible! It makes me sick! . . . When was it, Lou?"

"What's the difference?" I said. "I don't really remember. A long time ago."

I wished I'd kept my mouth shut about her not being pregnant. Now I couldn't back up on my story. She'd know I was lying and she'd be more suspicious than ever.

I grinned at her and walked my fingers up the curving plane of her belly. I squeezed one of her breasts, and then I moved my hand up until it was resting against her throat.

"What's the matter?" I said. "What have you got that pretty little face all puckered up for?"

She didn't say anything. She didn't smile back. She just lay there, staring, adding me up point by point, and she began to look more puzzled in one way and less in another. The answer was trying to crash through and it couldn't make it—quite. I was standing in the way. It couldn't get around the image she had of gentle, friendly easy-going Lou Ford.

"I think," she said slowly, "I'd better go home now."

"Maybe you'd better," I agreed. "It'll be dawn before long."

"Will I see you tomorrow? Today, I mean."

"Well, Saturday's a pretty busy day for me," I said. "I reckon we might go to church together Sunday or maybe have dinner together, but—"

"But you're busy Sunday night."

"I really am, honey. I promised to do a favor for a fellow, and I don't see how I can get out of it."

"I see. It never occurs to you to think about me when you're making all your plans, does it? Oh, no! I don't matter."

"I won't be tied up too long Sunday," I said. "Maybe until eleven o'clock or so. Why don't you come over and wait for me like you did tonight? I'd be tickled to death to have you."

Her eyes flickered, but she didn't break out with a lecture like she must have wanted to. She motioned for me to move so she could get up; and then she got up and began dressing.

"I'm awfully sorry, honey," I said.

"Are you?" She pulled her dress over her head, patted it down around her hips and buttoned the collar. Standing first on one foot then the other, she put on her pumps.

I got up and held her coat for her, smoothing it around her shoulders as I helped her into it.

She turned inside my arms and faced me. "All right, Lou," she said briskly. "We'll say no more tonight. But Sunday we'll have a good long talk. You're going to tell me why you've acted as you have these last few months, and no lying or evasions. Understand?"

"Ma'am, Miss Stanton," I said. "Yes, ma'am."

"All right," she nodded, "that's settled. Now you'd better put some clothes on or go back to bed before you catch cold."

5

That day, Saturday, was a busy one. There were a lot of payday drunks in town, it being the middle of the month, and drunks out here mean fights. All of us deputies and the two constables and Sheriff Maples had our hands full keeping things under control.

I don't have much trouble with drunks. Dad taught me they were touchy as all hell and twice as jumpy, and if you didn't ruffle 'em or alarm 'em they were the easiest people in the world to get along with. You should never bawl a drunk out, he said, because the guy had already bawled himself out to the breaking point. And you should never pull a gun or swing on a drunk because he was apt to feel that his life was in danger and act accordingly.

So I just moved around, friendly and gentle, taking the guys home wherever I could instead of to jail, and none of them got hurt and neither did I. But it all took time. From the time I went on at noon until eleven o'clock, I didn't so much as stop for a cup of coffee. Then around midnight, when I was already way over shift, I got one of the special jobs Sheriff Maples was always calling me in on.

A Mexican pipeliner had got all hayed up on marijuana and stabbed another Mexican to death. The boys had roughed him up pretty badly bringing him in and now, what with the hay and all, he was a regular wild man. They'd managed to get him off into one of the "quiet" cells, but the way he was cutting up he was going to take it apart or die in the attempt.

"Can't handle the crazy Mex the way we ought to," Sheriff Bob grumbled. "Not in a murder case. I miss my guess, we've already given some shyster defense lawyer enough to go yellin' third-degree."

"I'll see what I can do," I said.

I went down to the cell and I stayed there three hours, and I was busy every minute of it. I hardly had time to slam the door before the Mex dived at me. I caught his arms and held him back, letting him struggle and rave; and then I turned him loose and he dived again. I held him back again, turned him loose again. It went on and on.

I never slugged him or kicked him. I never let him struggle hard enough to hurt himself. I just wore him down, little by little, and when he quieted enough to hear me I began talking to him. Practically everyone in this area talks some Mex, but I do it better than most. I talked on and on, feeling him relax; and all the time I was wondering about myself.

This Mex, now, was about as defenseless as a man could be. He was hopped up and crazy. With the booting around he'd had, a little bit more would never have been noticed. I'd taken a lot bigger chance with what I'd done to that bum. The bum could have caused trouble. This Mex, alone in a cell with me, couldn't.

Yet I didn't so much as twist a finger. I'd never hurt a prisoner, someone that I could harm safely. I didn't have the slightest desire to. Maybe I had too much pride in my reputation for not using force. Or maybe I figured sub-consciously that the prisoners and I were on the same side. But however it was, I'd never hurt 'em. I didn't want to, and pretty soon I wouldn't want to hurt anyone. I'd get rid of her, and it would all be over for all time.

After three hours, like I say, the Mex was willing to behave. So I got him his clothes back and a blanket for his bunk, and let him smoke a cigarette while I tucked him in. Sheriff Maples peeped in as I was leaving, and shook his head wonderingly.

"Don't see how you do it, Lou," he swore. "Dagnab it, if I see where you get the patience."

"You've just got to keep smiling," I said. "That's the answer."

"Yeah? Do tell," he drawled.

"That's right," I said. "The man with the grin is the man who will win."

He gave me a funny look; and I laughed and slapped him on the back. "Just kidding, Bob," I said.

What the hell? You can't break a habit overnight. And what was the harm in a little kidding?

The sheriff wished me a good Sunday, and I drove on home. I fixed myself a big platter of ham and eggs and

French fries, and carried it into Dad's office. I ate at his desk, more at peace with myself than I'd been in a long time.

I'd made up my mind about one thing. Come hell or high water, I wasn't going to marry Amy Stanton. I'd been holding off on her account; I didn't feel I had the right to marry her. Now, though, I just wasn't going to do it. If I had to marry someone, it wouldn't be a bossy little gal with a tongue like barbed-wire and a mind about as narrow.

I carried my dishes into the kitchen, washed them up and took a long hot bath. Then I turned in and slept like a log until ten in the morning. While I was having breakfast, I heard gravel crunch in the driveway; and looking out I saw Chester Conway's Cadillac.

He came right in the house without knocking—people had got in the habit of that when Dad was practicing—and back into the kitchen.

"Keep your seat, boy, keep your seat," he said, though I hadn't made any move to get up. "Go right on with your breakfast."

"Thanks," I said.

He sat down, craning his neck so that he could look at the food on my plate. "Is that coffee fresh? I think I'll have some. Hop up and get me a cup, will you?"

"Yes, sir," I drawled. "Right away, Mr. Conway, sir."

That didn't faze him, of course; that was the kind of talk he felt he was entitled to. He took a noisy swill of coffee, then another. The third time he gulped the cup was emptied. He said he wouldn't take any more, without my offering him any, and lighted a cigar. He dropped the match on the floor, puffed and dusted ashes into his cup.

West Texans as a whole are a pretty high-handed lot, but they don't walk on a man if he stands up; they're quick to respect the other fellow's rights. Chester Conway was an exception. Conway had been *the* big man in town before the oil boom. He'd always been able to deal with others on his own terms. He'd gone without opposition for so many years that, by this time, he hardly knew it when he saw it. I believe I could have cussed him out in church and he wouldn't have turned a hair. He'd just have figured his ears were playing tricks on him.

It had never been hard for me to believe he'd arranged Mike's murder. The fact that *he* did it would automatically make it all right.

"Well," he said, dusting ashes all over the table. "Got everything fixed for tonight, have you? No chance of any slip-ups? You'll wind this thing right on up so it'll stay wound?"

"I'm not doing anything," I said. "I've done all I'm going to."

"Don't think we'd better leave it that way, Lou. 'Member I told you I didn't like the idea? Well, I still don't. That damned crazy Elmer sees her again no telling what'll happen. You take the money yourself, boy. I've got it all ready, ten thousand in small bills, and—"

"No," I said.

"—pay her off. Then bust her around a little, and run her across the county line."

"Mr. Conway," I said.

"That's the way to do it," he chuckled, his big pale jowls jouncing. "Pay her, bust her and chase her . . . You say something?"

I went through it again, real slowly, dealing it out a word at a time. Miss Lakeland insisted on seeing Elmer one more time before she left. She insisted on his bringing the dough, and she didn't want any witnesses along. Those were her terms, and if Conway wanted her to leave quietly he'd have to meet 'em. We could have her pinched, of course, but she was bound to talk if we did and it wouldn't be pretty talk.

Conway nodded irritably. "Understand all that. Can't have a lot of dirty publicity. But I don't see—"

"I'll tell you what you don't see, Mr. Conway," I said. "You don't see that you've got a hell of a lot of gall."

"Huh?" His mouth dropped open. "Wha-at?"

"I'm sorry," I said. "Stop and think a minute. How would it look if it got around that an officer of the law had made a blackmail payoff—that is, if she was willing to accept it from me? How do you think I feel being mixed up in a dirty affair of this kind? Now, Elmer got into this trouble and he came to me—"

"Only smart thing he ever did."

"—and I came to you. And you asked me to see what could be done about getting her out of town quietly. I did it. That's all I'm going to do. I don't see how you can ask me to do anything more."

"Well, uh"—he cleared his throat—"maybe not, boy. Reckon you're right. But you will see that she leaves after she gets the money?"

"I'll see to that," I said. "If she's not gone within an hour, I'll move her along myself."

He got up, fidgeting around nervously, so I walked him to the door to get rid of him. I couldn't take him much longer. It would have been bad enough if I hadn't known what he'd done to Mike.

I kept my hands in my pockets, pretending like I didn't see him when he started to shake hands. He opened the screen, then hesitated a moment.

"Better not go off anywhere," he said. "I'm sending Elmer over as soon as I can locate him. Want you to give him a good talking-to; see that he's got everything down straight. Make him know what's what, understand?"

"Yes, sir," I said. "It's mighty nice of you to let me talk to him."

"That's all right. No trouble at all," he said; and the screen slammed behind him.

A couple hours later Elmer showed up.

He was big and flabby-looking like his old man, and he tried to be as overbearing but he didn't quite have the guts for it. Some of our Central City boys had flattened him a few times, and it had done him a world of good. His blotched face was glistening with sweat; his breath would have tested a hundred and eighty proof.

"Getting started pretty early in the day, aren't you?" I said.

"So what?"

"Not a thing," I said. "I've tried to do you a favor. If you ball it up, it's your headache."

He grunted and crossed his legs. "I dunno, Lou," he frowned. "Dunno about all this. What if the old man never cools off? What'll me and Joyce do when the ten thousand runs out?"

"Well, Elmer," I said. "I guess there's some misunderstanding. I understood that you were sure your father would come around in time. If that isn't the case, maybe I'd better tell Miss Lakeland and—"

"No, Lou! Don't do that! . . . Hell, he'll get over it. He always gets over the things I do. But—"

"Why don't you do this?" I said. "Don't let your ten thousand run out. Buy you some kind of business; you and Joyce can run it together. When it's going good, get in touch with your Dad. He'll see that you've made a darned smart move, and you won't have any trouble squaring things."

Elmer brightened a little—doggoned little. Working wasn't Elmer's idea of a good solution to any problem.

"Don't let me talk you into it," I said. "I think Miss Lakeland has been mighty badly misjudged—she convinced me and I'm not easy to convince. I've stuck my neck out a mile to give you and her a fresh start together, but if you don't want to go—"

"Why'd you do it, Lou? Why'd you do all this for me and her?"

"Maybe money," I said, smiling. "I don't make very

much. Maybe I figured you'd do something for me in a money way."

His face turned a few shades redder. "Well . . . I could give you a little something out of the ten thousand, I guess."

"Oh, I wouldn't take any of that!" *You're damned right I wouldn't.* "I figured a man like you must have a little dough of his own. What do you do for your cigarettes and gas and whiskey? Does your Dad buy 'em for you?"

"Like hell!" He sat up and jerked out a roll of bills. "I got plenty of money."

He started to peel off a few bills—they were all twenties, it looked like—and then he caught my eye. I gave him a grin. It told him, plain as day, that I expected him to act like a cheapskate."

"Aw, hell," he said, and he wadded the roll together and tossed the whole thing to me. "See you tonight," he said, hoisting himself up.

"At ten o'clock," I nodded.

There were twenty-five twenties in the roll. Five hundred dollars. Now that I had it, it was welcome; I could always use a little extra money. But I hadn't planned on touching Elmer. I'd only done it to shut him up about my motives in helping him.

I didn't feel much like cooking, so I ate dinner in town. Coming home again I listened to the radio a while, read the Sunday papers and went to sleep.

Yes, maybe I was taking things pretty calmly, but I'd gone through the deal so often in my mind that I'd gotten used to it. *Joyce and Elmer were going to die. Joyce had*

*asked for it. The Conways had asked for it. I wasn't any
more cold-blooded than the dame who'd have me in hell
to get her own way. I wasn't any more cold-blooded than
the guy who'd had Mike knocked from an eight-story
building.*

Elmer hadn't done it, of course; probably he didn't even
know anything about it. But I had to get to the old man
through him. It was the only way I could, and it was the
way it should be. I'd be doing to him what he'd done to
Dad.

. . . It was eight o'clock when I waked up—eight of the
dark, moonless night I'd been waiting for. I gulped a cup
of coffee, eased the car down the alley and headed for
Derrick Road.

6

Here in the oil country you see quite a few places like the old Branch house. They were ranch houses or homesteads at one time; but wells were drilled around 'em, right up to their doorsteps sometimes, and everything nearby became a mess of oil and sulphur water and red sun-baked drilling mud. The grease-black grass dies. The creeks and springs disappear. And then the oil is gone and the houses stand black and abandoned, lost and lonely looking behind the pest growths of sunflowers and sage and Johnson grass.

The Branch place stood back from Derrick Road a few hundred feet, at the end of a lane so overgrown with weeds that I almost missed it. I turned into the lane, killed the motor after a few yards and got out.

At first I couldn't see a thing; it was that dark. But gradually my eyes became used to it. I could see all I needed to see. I opened the trunk compartment and located a tire tool. Taking a rusty spike from my pocket, I drove it into the right rear tire. There was a *poof!* and a *whish-ss!* The springs squeaked and whined as the car settled rapidly.

I got a jack under the axle, and raised it a foot or so. I rocked the car and slid it off the jack. I left it that way and headed up the lane.

It took maybe five minutes to reach the house and pull a plank from the porch. I leaned it against the gate post where I could find it in a hurry, and headed across the fields to Joyce's house.

"Lou!" She stood back from the door, startled. "I couldn't imagine who—where's your car? Is something wrong?"

"Nothing but a flat tire," I grinned. "I had to leave the car down the road a piece."

I sauntered into the living room, and she came around in front of me, gripping her arms around my back and pressing her face against my shirt. Her negligee fell open, accidentally on purpose I imagine. She moved her body against mine.

"Lou, honey . . ."

"Yeah?" I said.

"It's only about nine and Stupid won't be here for another hour, and I won't see you for two weeks. And . . . well, you know."

I knew. I knew how *that* would look in an autopsy.

"Well, I don't know, baby," I said. "I'm kind of pooped out, and you're all prettied up—"

"Oh, I am not!" She squeezed me. "I'm always prettied up to hear you tell it. Hurry, so I can have my bath."

Bath. That made it okay. "You twisted my arm, baby," I said, and I swept her up and carried her into the bedroom. And, no, it didn't bother me a bit.

Because right in the middle of it, right in the middle of the sweet talk and sighing, she suddenly went still and pushed my head back and looked me in the eye.

"You *will* join me in two weeks, Lou? Just as soon as you sell your house and wind up your affairs?"

"That's the understanding," I said.

"Don't keep me waiting. I want to be sweet to you, but if you won't let me I'll be the other way. I'll come back here and raise hell. I'll follow you around town and tell everyone how you—"

"—robbed you of your bloom and cast you aside?" I said.

"Crazy!" she giggled. "But just the same, Lou . . ."

"I know. I won't keep you waiting, baby."

I lay on the bed while she had her bath. She came back in from it, wiping herself with a big towel, and got some panties and a brassiere out of a suitcase. She stepped into the panties, humming, and brought the brassiere over to me. I helped her put it on, giving her a pinch or two, and she giggled and wiggled.

I'm going to miss you, baby, I thought. You've got to go, but I'm sure going to miss you.

"Lou . . . You suppose Elmer will make any trouble?"

"I already told you," I said. "What can he do? He can't squawk to his Dad. I'll tell him I changed my mind, and we'll have to keep faith with the old man. And that'll be that."

She frowned. "It seems so—oh, so complicated! I mean it looks like we could have got the money without dragging Elmer into it."

"Well. . . ." I glanced at the clock.

Nine-thirty-three. I didn't need to stall any longer. I sat up beside her, swinging my feet to the floor; casually drawing on my gloves.

"Well, I'll tell you, baby," I said. "It *is* kind of complicated, but it has to be that way. You've probably heard the gossip about Mike Dean, my foster brother? Well, Mike didn't do that. He took the blame for me. So if you should do your talking around town, it would be a lot worse than you realized. People would start thinking, and before it was all over . . ."

"But, Lou. I'm not going to say anything. You're going to join me and—"

"Better let me finish," I said. "I told you how Mike fell from that building? Only he didn't fall; he was murdered. Old man Conway arranged it and—"

"Lou"—she didn't get it at all. "I won't let you do anything to Elmer! You mustn't, honey. They'll catch you and you'll go to jail and—oh, honey, don't even think about it!"

"They won't catch me," I said. "They won't even suspect me. They'll think he was half-stiff, like he usually is, and you got to fighting and both got killed."

She still didn't get it. She laughed, frowning a little at the same time. "But, Lou—that doesn't make sense. How could I be dead when—"

"Easy," I said, and I gave her a slap. And still she didn't get it.

She put a hand to her face and rubbed it slowly. "Y-you'd better not do that, now, Lou. I've got to travel, and—"

"You're not going anywhere, baby," I said, and I hit her again.

And at last she got it.

She jumped up and I jumped with her. I whirled her around and gave her a quick one-two, and she shot backwards across the room and bounced and slumped against the wall. She staggered to her feet, weaving, mumbling, and half-fell toward me. I let her have it again.

I backed her against the wall, slugging, and it was like pounding a pumpkin. Hard, then everything giving away at once. She slumped down, her knees bent under her, her head hanging limp; and then, slowly, an inch at a time, she pushed herself up again.

She couldn't see; I don't know how she could. I don't know how she could stand or go on breathing. But she brought her head up, wobbling, and she raised her arms, raised them and spread them and held them out. And then she staggered toward me, just as a car pulled into the yard.

"Guhguh-guhby . . . kiss guhguh-guh—"

I brought an uppercut up from the floor. There was a sharp *cr-aack!* and her whole body shot upward, and came down in a heap. And that time it stayed down.

I wiped my gloves on her body; it was her blood and it belonged there. I took the gun from the dresser, turned off the light and closed the door.

Elmer was coming up the steps, crossing the porch. I got to the front door and opened it.

"Hiya, Lou, ol' boy, ol' boy, ol' boy," he said. "Right on time, huh? Thass Elmer Conway, always right on time."

"Half-stiff," I said, "that's Elmer Conway. Have you got the money?"

He patted the thick brown folder under his arm. "What's it look like? Where's Joyce?"

"Back in the bedroom. Why don't you go on back? I'll bet she won't say no if you try to slip it to her."

"Aw," he blinked foolishly. "Aw, you shouldn't talk like that, Lou. You know we're gonna get married."

"Suit yourself," I shrugged. "I'd bet money though that she's all stretched out waiting for you."

I wanted to laugh out loud. I wanted to yell. I wanted to leap on him and tear him to pieces.

"Well, maybe . . ."

He turned suddenly and lumbered down the hall. I leaned against the wall, waiting, as he entered the bedroom and turned on the light.

I heard him say, "Hiya, Joyce, ol' kid, ol' ol' ol' k-k-k . . ." I heard a heavy thump, and a gurgling, strangled sound. Then he said, he screamed, "Joyce . . . Joyce . . . *Lou!*"

I sauntered back. He was down on his knees and there was blood on his hands, and a big streak across his chin where he'd wiped it. He looked up at me, his mouth hanging open.

I laughed—I had to laugh or do something worse—and his eyes squeezed shut and he bawled. I yelled with laughter, bending over and slapping my legs. I doubled up, laughing and farting and laughing some more. Until there wasn't a laugh in me or anyone. I'd used up all the laughter in the world.

He got to his feet, smearing his face with his big flabby hands, staring at me stupidly.

"W-who did it, Lou?"

"It was suicide," I said. "A plain case of suicide."

"B-but that d-don't make—"

"It's the only thing that does make sense! It was the way it was, you hear me? Suicide, you hear me? Suicide suicide suicide! I didn't kill her. Don't you say I killed her. SHE KILLED HERSELF!"

I shot him, then, right in his gaping stupid mouth. I emptied the gun into him.

Stooping, I curved Joyce's hand around the gun butt, then dropped the gun at her side. I went out the door and across the fields again, and I didn't look back.

I found the plank and carried it down to my car. If the car had been seen, that plank was my alibi. I'd had to go up and find one to put under the jack.

I ran the jack up on the plank and put on the spare tire. I threw the tools into the car, started the motor and backed toward Derrick Road. Ordinarily, I'd no more back into a highway at night without my lights than I would without my pants. But this wasn't ordinarily. I just didn't think of it.

If Chester Conway's Cadillac had been traveling faster, I wouldn't be writing this.

He swarmed out of his car cursing, saw who I was, and cursed harder than ever. "Goddamit, Lou, you know better'n that! You trying to get killed, for Christ's sake? Huh? What the hell are you doing here, anyhow?"

"I had to pull in there with a flat tire," I said. "Sorry if I—"

"Well, come on. Let's get going. Can't stand here gabbing at night."

"Going?" I said. "It's still early."

"The hell it is! It's a quarter past eleven, and that damned Elmer ain't home yet. Promised to come right back, and he ain't done it. Probably up there working himself into another scrape."

"Maybe we'd better give him a little more time," I said. I had to wait a while. I couldn't go back in that house now. "Why don't you go on home, Mr. Conway, and I'll—"

"I'm going now!" He turned away from the car. "And you follow me!"

The door of the Cadillac slammed. He backed up and pulled around me, yelling again for me to come on. I yelled back that I would and he drove off. Fast.

I got a cigar lit. I started the motor and killed it. I started it and killed it again. Finally, it stayed running, it just wouldn't die, so I drove off.

I drove up the lane at Joyce's house and parked at the end of it. There wasn't room in the yard with Elmer's and the old man's cars there. I shut off the motor and got out. I climbed the steps and crossed the porch.

The door was open and he was in the living room, talking on the telephone. And his face was like a knife had come down it, slicing away all the flabbiness.

He didn't seem very excited. He didn't seem very sad. He was just businesslike, and somehow that made it worse.

"Sure, it's too bad," he said. "Don't tell me that again. I know all about how bad it is. He's dead and that's that, and what I'm interested in is her. . . . Well, do it then! Get on out here. We ain't going to let her die, get me? Not this way. I'm going to see that she burns."

7

It was almost three o'clock in the morning when I got through talking—answering questions, mostly—to Sheriff Maples and the county attorney, Howard Hendricks; and I guess you know I wasn't feeling so good. I was kind of sick to my stomach, and I felt, well, pretty damned sore, angry. Things shouldn't have turned out this way. It was just plumb unreasonable. It wasn't right.

I'd done everything I could to get rid of a couple of undesirable citizens in a neat no-kickbacks way. And here one of 'em was still alive; and purple hell was popping about the other one.

Leaving the courthouse, I drove to the Greek's place and got a cup of coffee that I didn't want. His boy had taken a part-time job in a filling station, and the old man wasn't sure whether it was a good thing or not. I promised to drop by and look in on the lad.

I didn't want to go home and answer a lot more questions from Amy. I hoped that if I stalled long enough, she'd give up and leave.

Johnnie Pappas, the Greek's boy, was working at Slim

Murphy's place. He was around at the side of the station when I drove in, doing something to the motor of his hot rod. I got out of my car and he came toward me slowly, sort of watchfully, wiping his hands on a chunk of waste.

"Just heard about your new job, Johnnie," I said. "Congratulations."

"Yeah." He was tall, good-looking; not at all like his father. "Dad send you out here?"

"He told me you'd gone to work here," I said. "Anything wrong with that?"

"Well . . . You're up pretty late."

"Well," I laughed, "so are you. Now how about filling 'er up with gas and checking the oil?"

He got busy, and by the time he was through he'd pretty much lost his suspicions. "I'm sorry if I acted funny, Lou. Dad's been kind of nagging me—he just can't understand that a guy my age needs a little real dough of his own— and I thought he was having you check up on me."

"You know me better than that, Johnnie."

"Sure, I do," he smiled, warmly. "I've got plenty of nagging from people, but no one but you ever really tried to help me. You're the only real friend I've ever had in this lousy town. Why do you do it, Lou? What's the percentage in bothering with a guy that everyone else is down on?"

"Oh, I don't know," I said. And I didn't. I didn't even know how I could stand here talking to him with the terrible load I had on my mind. "Maybe it's because I was a kid myself not so many years ago. Fathers are funny. The best ones get in your hair most."

"Yeah. Well . . ."

"What hours do you work, Johnnie?"

"Just midnight to seven, Saturdays and Sundays. Just enough to keep me in pocket money. Dad thinks I'll be too tired to go to school on Mondays, but I won't, Lou. I'll make it fine."

"Sure, you will," I said. "There's just one thing, Johnnie. Slim Murphy hasn't got a very good reputation. We've never proved that he was mixed up in any of these car-stripping jobs, but . . ."

"I know." He kicked the gravel of the driveway, uncomfortably. "I won't get into any trouble, Lou."

"Good enough," I said. "That's a promise, and I know you don't break your promises."

I paid him with a twenty dollar bill, got my change and headed toward home. Wondering about myself. Shaking my head, as I drove. I hadn't put on an act. I *was* concerned and worried about the kid. Me, worried about *his* troubles.

The house was all dark when I got home, but it would be, whether Amy was there or not. So I didn't get my hopes too high. I figured that my standing her up would probably make her all the more determined to stay; that she was a cinch to crop up at the one time I didn't want any part of her. That's the way I figured it, and that's the way it was.

She was up in my bedroom in bed. And she'd filled two ashtrays with the cigarettes she'd smoked. And mad! I've never seen one little old girl so mad in my life.

I sat down on the edge of the bed and pulled off my boots; and for about the next twenty minutes I didn't say a word. I didn't get a chance. Finally, she began to slow up a little, and I tried to apologize.

"I'm sure sorry, honey, but I couldn't help it. I've had a lot of trouble tonight."

"I'll bet!"

"You want to hear about it or not? If you don't, just say so."

"Oh, go on! I've heard so many of your lies and excuses I may as well hear a few more."

I told her what had happened—that is, what was *supposed* to have happened—and she could hardly hold herself in until I'd finished. The last word was hardly out of my mouth before she'd cut loose on me again.

"How could you be so stupid, Lou? How *could* you do it? Getting yourself mixed up with some wretched prostitute and that awful Elmer Conway! Now, there'll be a big scandal and you'll probably lose your job, and—"

"Why?" I mumbled. "I didn't do anything."

"I want to know why you did it!"

"Well, it was kind of a favor, see? Chester Conway wanted me to see what I could do about getting Elmer out of this scrape, so—"

"Why did he have to come to you? Why do you always have to be doing favors for other people? You never do any for me!"

I didn't say anything for a minute. But I thought, *That's*

what you think, honey. I'm doing you a favor by not beating your head off.

"Answer me, Lou Ford!"

"All right," I said. "I shouldn't have done it."

"You shouldn't have allowed that woman to stay in this county in the first place!"

"No," I nodded. "I shouldn't have."

"Well?"

"I'm not perfect," I snapped. "I make plenty of mistakes. How many times do you want me to say it?"

"Well! All I've got to say is . . ."

All she had to say would take her the rest of her life to finish; and I wasn't even halfway in the mood for it. I reached out and grabbed her by the crotch.

"Lou! You stop that!"

"Why?" I said.

"Y-you stop it!" She shivered. "You s-stop or . . . Oh *Lou!*"

I lay down beside her with my clothes on. I had to do it, because there was just one way of shutting Amy up.

So I laid down and she swarmed up against me. And there wasn't a thing wrong with Amy when she was like that; you couldn't have asked much more from a woman. But there was plenty wrong with me. Joyce Lakeland was wrong with me.

"Lou . . ." Amy slowed down a little. "What's the matter, dear?"

"All this trouble," I said. "I guess it's thrown me for a loop."

"You poor darling. Just forget everything but me, and I'll pet you and whisper to you, mmm? I'll . . ." She kissed me and whispered what she would do. And she did it. And, hell, she might as well have done it to a fence post.

Baby Joyce had taken care of me, but good.

Amy pulled her hand away, and began brushing it against her hip. Then she snatched up a handful of sheet, and wiped—scrubbed—her hip with it.

"You son-of-a-bitch," she said. "You dirty, filthy bastard."

"Wha-at?" I said. It was like getting a punch in the guts. Amy didn't go in for cussing. At least, I'd never heard her do much.

"You're dirty. I can tell. I can smell it on you. Smell her. You can't wash it off. It'll never come off. You—"

"Jesus Christ!" I grabbed her by the shoulders. "What are you saying, Amy?"

"You screwed her. You've been doing it all along. You've been putting her dirty insides inside of me, smearing me with her. And I'm going to make you pay for it. If it's the l-last thing I ever d-do, I'll—"

She jerked away from me, sobbing, and jumped out of bed. As I got up, she backed around a chair, putting it between me and her.

"K-keep away from me! Don't you dare touch me!"

"Why, sure, honey," I said. "Whatever you say."

She didn't see the meaning yet of what she'd said. All she could think of was herself, the insult to herself. But I knew that, given enough time—and not much at that—she'd put all the parts of the picture together. She wouldn't have any real proof, of course. All she had to go on was guesswork—intuition—and that operation I'd had: something, thank God, which seemed to have slipped her mind for the moment. Anyway, she'd talk. And the fact that there wasn't any proof for what she said, wouldn't help me much.

You don't need proof, know what I mean? Not from what I've seen of the law in operation. All you need is a tip that a guy is guilty. From then on, unless he's a big shot, it's just a matter of making him admit it.

"Amy," I said. "Amy, honey. Look at me."

"I d-don't want to look at you."

"Look at me. . . . This is Lou, honey, Lou Ford, remember? The guy you've known all your life. I ask you, now, would I do what you said I did?"

She hesitated, biting her lips. "You did do it." Her voice was just a shade uncertain. "I know you did."

"You don't know anything," I said. "Just because I'm tired and upset, you jump to a crazy conclusion. Why, why would I fool around with some chippy when I had you? What could a dame like that give me that would make me run the risk of losing a girl like you? Huh? Now, that doesn't make sense, does it, honey."

"Well . . ." That had got to her. It had hit her right in the pride, where she was tenderest. But it wasn't quite enough to jar her loose from her hunch.

She picked up her panties and began putting them on, still standing behind the chair. "There's no use arguing about it, Lou," she said, wearily. "I suppose I can thank my lucky stars that I haven't caught some terrible disease."

"But dammit . . . !" I moved around the chair, suddenly, and got her in my arms. "Dammit, stop talking that way about the girl I'm going to marry! I don't mind for myself, but you can't say it about her, get me? You can't say that the girl I'm going to marry would sleep with a guy who plays around with whores!"

"Let me go, Lou! Let . . ." She stopped struggling, abruptly.

"What did you—?"

"You heard me," I said.

"B-but just two days ago—"

"So what?" I said. "No man likes to be yanked into marriage. He wants to do his own proposing, which is just what I'm doing right now. Hell, we've already put it off too long, in my opinion. This crazy business tonight proves it. If we were married we wouldn't have all these quarrels and misunderstandings like we've been having."

"Since that woman came to town, you mean."

"All right," I said. "I've done all I could. If you're willing to believe that about me, I wouldn't want—"

"Wait, Lou!" She hung on to me. "After all, you can't blame me if—" And she let it go at that. She had to give up for her own sake. "I'm sorry, Lou. Of course, I was wrong."

"You certainly were."

"When shall we do it, Lou? Get married, I mean."

"The sooner the better," I lied. I didn't have the slightest intention of marrying her. But I needed time to do some planning, and I had to keep her quiet. "Let's get together in a few days when we're both more ourselves, and talk about it."

"Huh-uh." She shook her head. "Now that you've—we've come to the decision, let's go through with it. Let's talk about it right now."

"But it's getting daylight, honey," I said. "If you're still here even a little while from now, people will see you when you leave."

"I don't care if they do, darling. I don't care a teensy-weensie little bit." She snuggled against me, burrowing her head against my chest. And without seeing her face, I knew she was grinning. She had me on the run, and she was getting a hell of a kick out of it.

"Well, I'm pretty tired," I said. "I think I ought to sleep a little while before—"

"I'll make you some coffee, darling. That'll wake you up."

"But, honey—"

The phone rang. She let go of me, not very hurriedly, and I stepped over to the writing desk and picked up the extension.

"Lou?" It was Sheriff Bob Maples.

"Yeah, Bob," I said. "What's on your mind?"

He told me, and I said, Okay, and hung up the phone again. Amy looked at me, and changed her mind about popping off.

"Your job, Lou? You've got some work to do?"

"Yeah," I nodded. "Sheriff Bob's driving by to pick me up in a few moments."

"You poor dear! And you so tired! I'll get dressed and get right out."

I helped her dress, and walked to the back door with her. She gave me a couple of big kisses and I promised to call her as soon as I got a chance. She left then, a couple of minutes before Sheriff Maples drove up.

8

The county attorney, Howard Hendricks, was with him, sitting in the back seat of the car. I gave him a cold-eyed look and a nod, as I got in the front, and he gave me back the look without a nod. I'd never had much use for him. He was one of those professional patriots, always talking about what a great hero he'd been in the war.

Sheriff Bob put the car in gear, clearing his throat uncomfortably. "Sure hated to bother you, Lou," he said. "Hope I didn't interrupt anything."

"Nothing that can't wait," I said. "She—I'd already kept her waiting five-six hours."

"You had a date for last night?" asked Hendricks.

"That's right"—I didn't turn around in the seat.

"For what time?"

"For a little after ten. The time I figured I'd have the Conway business finished."

The county attorney grunted. He sounded more than a mite disappointed. "Who was the girl?"

"None of your—"

"Wait a minute, Lou!" Bob eased his foot off the gas, and turned onto Derrick Road. "Howard, you're getting way out of line. You're kind of a newcomer out this way—been here eight years now, ain't you?—but you still ought to know better'n to ask a man a question like that."

"What the hell?" said Hendricks. "It's my job. It's an important question. If Ford had himself a date last night, it—well"—he hesitated—"it shows that he planned on being there instead of—well, uh—some place else. You see what I mean, Ford?"

I saw, all right, but I wasn't going to tell him so. I was just old dumb Lou from Kalamazoo. I wouldn't be thinking about an alibi, because I hadn't done anything to need an alibi for.

"No," I drawled, "I reckon I don't know what you mean. To come right down to cases, and no offense meant, I figured you'd done all the jawing you had to do when I talked to you an hour or so ago."

"Well, you're dead wrong, brother!" He glared at me, red-faced, in the rearview mirror. "I've got quite a few more questions. And I'm still waiting for the answer to the last one I asked. Who was the—"

"Drop it, Howard!" Bob jerked his head curtly. "Don't ask Lou that again, or I'm personally going to lose my temper. I know the girl. I know her folks. She's one of the nicest little ladies in town, and I ain't got the slightest doubt Lou had a date with her."

Hendricks scowled, gave out with an irritated laugh. "I don't get it. She's not too nice to sl—well, skip it—but she's too nice to have her name mentioned in the strictest confidence. I'm damned if I can understand a deal like that. The more I'm around you people the less I can understand you."

I turned around, smiling, looking friendly and serious. For a while, anyway, it wasn't a good idea to have anyone sore at me. And a guy that's got something on his conscience can't afford to get riled.

"I guess we're a pretty stiff-necked lot out here, Howard," I said. "I suppose it comes from the fact that this country was never very thickly settled, and a man had to be doggoned careful of the way he acted or he'd be marked for life. I mean, there wasn't any crowd for him to sink into—he was always out where people could see him."

"So?"

"So if a man or woman does something, nothing bad you understand, but the kind of thing men and women have always been doing, you don't let on that you know anything about it. You don't, because sooner or later you're going to need the same kind of favor yourself. You see how it is? It's the only way we can go on being human, and still hold our heads up."

He nodded indifferently. "Very interesting. Well, here we are, Bob."

Sheriff Maples pulled off the pavement and parked on the shoulder of the road. We got out, and Hendricks nodded toward the weed-grown trail which led up to the old Branch house. He jerked his head at it, and then turned and looked at me.

"Do you see that track through there, Ford? Do you know what caused that?"

"Why, I reckon so," I said. "A flat tire."

"You admit that? You concede that a track of that kind would have to be there, *if* you had a flat tire?"

I pushed back my Stetson, and scratched my head. I looked at Bob, frowning a little. "I don't guess I see what you boys are driving at," I said. "What's this all about, Bob?"

Of course, I did see. I saw that I'd made one hell of a bonehead play. I'd guessed it as soon as I saw the track through the weeds, and I had an answer ready. But I couldn't come out with it too fast. It had to be done easy-like.

"This is Howard's show," said the sheriff. "Maybe you'd better answer him, Lou."

"Okay," I shrugged. "I've already said it once. A flat tire makes that kind of track."

"Do you know," said Hendricks slowly, "when that track was made?"

"I ain't got the slightest idea," I said. "All I know is that my car didn't make it."

"You're a damned li—*Huh?*" Hendrick's mouth dropped open foolishly. "B-but—"

"I didn't have a flat when I turned off the highway."

"Now, wait a minute! You—"

"Maybe you better wait a minute," Sheriff Bob interrupted. "I don't recollect Lou tellin' us his tire went flat here on Derrick Road. Don't recall his sayin' anything of the kind."

"If I did say it," I said, "I sure as heck didn't mean to. I knew I had a puncture, sure; I felt the car sway a little. But I turned off in the lane before the tire could really go down."

Bob nodded and glanced at Hendricks. The county attorney suddenly got busy lighting a cigarette. I don't know which was redder—his face or the sun pushing up over the hills.

I scratched my head again. "Well," I said, "I reckon it's none of my business. But I sure hope you fellows didn't chew up a good tire makin' that track."

Hendricks' mouth was working. Bob's old eyes sparkled. Off in the distance somewhere, maybe three-four miles away, there was a *suck-whush* as a mudhog drilling pump began to growl. Suddenly, the sheriff whuffed and coughed and let out a wild whoop of laughter.

"Haw, haw, haw!" he boomed. "Doggone it, Howard, if this ain't the funniest—haw, haw, haw—"

And then, Hendricks started laughing, too. Restrained, uncomfortable, at first; then, plain unashamed laughter. I stood looking on, grinning puzzledly, like a guy who wanted to join in but didn't know the score.

I was glad now that I'd made that bonehead mistake. When a man's rope slides off you once, he's mighty cautious about making a second throw.

Hendricks slapped me on the back. "I'm a damned fool, Lou. I should have known better."

"Say," I said, letting it dawn on me at last. "You don't mean you thought I—"

"Of course, we didn't think so," said Bob, warmly. "Nothing of the kind."

"It was just something that had to be looked into," Hendricks explained. "We had to have an answer for it. Now, you didn't talk much to Conway last night, did you?"

"No," I said. "It didn't seem to me like a very good time to do much talking."

"Well, I talked to him, Bob, I did. Rather he talked to us. And he's really raring and tearing. This woman—what's her name, Lakeland?—is as good as dead. The doctors say she'll never regain consciousness, so Conway isn't going to be able to lay the blame for this mess on her. Naturally, then, he'll want to stick someone else with it; he'll be snatching at straws. That's why we have to head him off on anything that looks—uh—even mildly peculiar."

"But, shucks," I said, "anyone could see what happened. Elmer'd been drinking, and he tried to push her around, and—"

"Sure. But Conway don't want to admit that. And he won't admit it, if there's any way out."

We all rode in the front seat going back to town. I was in the middle, squeezed in between the sheriff and Hendricks; and all of a sudden a crazy notion came over me. Maybe I hadn't fooled 'em. Maybe they were putting on an act, just like I was. Maybe that was why they'd put me in the middle, so I couldn't jump out of the car.

It was a crazy idea, of course, and it was gone in a moment. But I started a little before I could catch myself.

"Feelin' twitchy?" said Bob.

"Just hunger pains," I grinned. "I haven't eaten since yesterday afternoon."

"Wouldn't mind a bite myself," Bob nodded. "How about you, Howard?"

"Might be a good idea. Mind stopping by the court-house first?"

"Huh-uh," said Bob. "We go by there and we're apt not to get away. You can call from the restaurant—call my office, too, while you're at it."

Word of what had happened was already all over town, and there was a lot of whispering and gawking as we pulled up in front of the restaurant. I mean, there was a lot of whispering and gawking from the newcomers, the oil workers and so on. The old timers just nodded and went on about their business.

Hendricks stopped to use the telephone, and Bob and I sat down in a booth. We ordered ham and eggs all around, and pretty soon Hendricks came back.

"That Conway!" he snapped, sliding in across from us. "Now he wants to fly that woman into Fort Worth. Says she can't get the right kind of medical attention here."

"Yeah?" Bob looked down at the menu, casually. "What time is he takin' her?"

"I'm not at all sure that he is! I'm the man that has the say-so on handling this case. Why, she hasn't even been booked yet, let alone arraigned. We haven't had a chance."

"Can't see that it makes much difference," said Bob, "as long as she's going to die."

"That's not the point! The point is—"

"Yeah, sure," drawled Bob. "You like to take a little trip into Fort Worth, Lou? Maybe I'll go along myself."

"Why, I guess I could," I said.

"I reckon we'll do that, then. Okay, Howard? That'll take care of the technicalities for you."

The waitress set food in front of us, and Bob picked up his knife and fork. I felt his boot kick mine under the table. Hendricks knew how things stood, but he was too much of a phoney to admit it. He had to go on playing the big hero—the county attorney that didn't take orders from anyone.

"Now, see here, Bob. Maybe I'm new here, as you see it; maybe I've got a lot to learn. But, by God, I know the law and—"

"So do I," the sheriff nodded. "The one that ain't on the books. Conway wasn't asking you if he could take her to Fort Worth. He was telling you. Did he mention what time?"

"Well"—Hendricks swallowed heavily—"ten this morning, he thought. He wanted to—he's chartering one of the airline's twin-motor jobs, and they've got to fit it up with oxygen and a—"

"Uh-huh. Well, that ought to be all right. Lou and me'll have time to scrub up a little and pack a bag. I'll drop you off at your place, Lou, as soon as we finish here."

"Fine," I said.

Hendricks didn't say anything.

After a minute or two, Bob glanced at him and raised his eyebrows. "Something wrong with your eggs, son? Better eat 'em before they get cold."

Hendricks heaved a sigh, and began to eat.

Bob and I were at the airport quite a bit ahead of time, so we went ahead and got on the plane and made ourselves comfortable. Some workmen were pounding around in the baggage compartment, fixing things up according to the doctor's instructions, but tired as we were it would have taken more than that to keep us awake. Bob began to nod, first. Then I closed my eyes, figuring to just rest them a little. And I guess I must have gone right to sleep. I didn't even know when we took off.

One minute I was closing my eyes. The next, it seemed like, Bob was shaking me and pointing out the window.

"There she is, Lou. There's cow town."

I looked out and down. I felt kind of disappointed. I'd never been out of the county before, and now that I was sure Joyce wasn't going to live I could have enjoyed seeing the sights. As it was I hadn't seen anything. I'd wasted all my time sleeping.

"Where's Mr. Conway?" I asked.

"Back in the baggage compartment. I just went back for a look myself."

"She—she's still unconscious?"

"Uh-huh, and she ain't ever going to be any other way if you ask me." He shook his head solemnly. "Conway don't know when he's well off. If that no-account Elmer wasn't already dead, he'd be swingin' from a tree about now."

"Yeah," I said. "It's pretty bad all right."

"Don't know what would possess a man to do a thing like that. Dogged if I do! Don't see how he could be drunk enough or mean enough to do it."

"I guess it's my fault," I said. "I shouldn't have ever let her stay in town."

"We-el . . . I told you to use your own judgment, and she was a mighty cute little trick from all I hear. I'd probably have let her stay myself if I'd been in your place."

"I'm sure sorry, Bob," I said. "I sure wish I'd come to you instead of trying to handle this blackmail deal myself."

"Yeah," he nodded slowly, "but I reckon we've been over that ground enough. It's done now, and there's nothing we can do about it. Talking and fretting about might-have-beens won't get us anywhere."

"No," I said. "I guess there's no use crying over spilled milk."

The plane began to circle and lose altitude, and we fastened our seat belts. A couple of minutes later we were skimming along the landing field, and a police car and ambulance were keeping pace with us.

The plane stopped, and the pilot came out of his compartment and unlocked the door. Bob and I got out, and

watched while the doctor supervised the unloading of the
stretcher. The upper part of it was closed in kind of a
little tent, and all I could see was the outline of her body
under the sheet. Then I couldn't even see that; they were
hustling her off toward the ambulance. And a heavy hand
came down on my shoulder.

"Lou," said Chester Conway. "You come with me in
the police car."

"Well," I said, glancing at Bob. "I kind of figured
on—"

"You come with me," he repeated. "Sheriff, you ride
in the ambulance. We'll see you at the hospital."

Bob pushed back his Stetson, and gave him a hard
sharp look. Then his face sort of sagged and he turned
and walked away, his scuffed boots dragging against the
pavement.

I'd been pretty worried about how to act around Conway. Now, seeing the way he'd pushed old Bob Maples
around, I was just plain sore. I jerked away from his
hand and got into the police car. I kept my head turned
as Conway climbed in and slammed the door.

The ambulance started up, and headed off the field.
We followed it. Conway leaned forward and closed the
glass partition between our seat and the driver's.

"Didn't like that, did you?" he grunted. "Well, there
may be a lot of things you don't like before this is over.
I've got the reputation of my dead boy at stake, understand? My own reputation. I'm looking out for that and
nothing but that, and I ain't standing on etiquette. I'm
not letting someone's tender feelings get in my way."

"I don't suppose you would," I said. "It'd be pretty hard to start in at your time of life."

I wished, immediately, that I hadn't said it; I was giving myself away, you see. But he didn't seem to have heard me. Like always, he wasn't hearing anything he didn't want to hear.

"They're operating on that woman as soon as she gets to the hospital," he went on. "If she pulls through the operation, she'll be able to talk by tonight. I want you there at that time—just as soon as she comes out of the anesthetic."

"Well?" I said.

"Bob Maples is all right, but he's too old to be on his toes. He's liable to foul up the works right when you need him most. That's why I'm letting him go on now when it don't matter whether anyone's around or not."

"I don't know as I understand you," I said. "You mean—"

"I've got rooms reserved at a hotel. I'll drop you off there, and you stay there until I call you. Get some rest, understand? Get rested up good, so's you'll be on your toes and raring to go when the time comes."

"All right," I shrugged, "but I slept all the way up on the plane."

"Sleep some more, then. You may have to be up all night."

The hotel was on West Seventh Street, a few blocks from the hospital; and Conway had engaged a whole suite of rooms. The assistant manager of the place went up with me and the bellboy, and a couple of minutes after they left a waiter brought in a tray of whiskey and ice. And right behind him came another waiter with a flock of sandwiches and coffee.

I poured myself a nice drink, and took it over by the window. I sat down in a big easy chair, and propped my boots up on the radiator. I leaned back, grinning.

Conway was a big shot, all right. He could push you around and make you like it. He could have places like this, with people jumping sideways to wait on him. He could have everything but what he wanted—his son and a good name.

His son had beaten a whore to death, and she'd killed him; and he'd never be able to live it down. Not if he lived to be a hundred and I damned well hoped he would.

I ate part of a clubhouse sandwich, but it didn't seem to set so well. So I fixed another big drink and took it over to the window. I felt kind of restless and uneasy. I wished I could get out and wander around the town.

Fort Worth is the beginning of West Texas, and I wouldn't have felt conspicuous, dressed as I was, like I would have in Dallas or Houston. I could have had a fine time—seen something new for a change. And instead I had to stay here by myself, doing nothing, seeing nothing, thinking the same old thoughts.

It was like there was a plot against me almost. I'd done something wrong, way back when I was a kid, and I'd never been able to get away from it. I'd had my nose rubbed in it day after day until, like an overtrained dog, I'd started crapping out of pure fright. And, now, here I was—

I poured another drink. . . .

—Here I was, now, but it wouldn't be like this much longer. Joyce was bound to die if she wasn't dead already. I'd got rid of her and I'd got rid of *it*—the sickness—when I did it. And just as soon as things quieted down, I'd quit my job and sell the house and Dad's practice and pull out.

Amy Stanton? Well—I shook my head—she wasn't going to stop me. She wasn't going to keep me chained there in Central City. I didn't know just how I'd break away from her, but I knew darned well that I would.

Some way. Somehow.

More or less to kill time, I took a long hot bath; and afterwards I tried the sandwiches and coffee again. I paced around the room, eating and drinking coffee, moving from window to window. I wished we weren't up so high so's I could see a little something.

I tried taking a nap, and that was no good. I got a shine cloth out of the bathroom and began rubbing at my boots. I'd got one brushed up real good and was starting on the toe of the second when Bob Maples came in.

He said hello, casually, and fixed himself a drink. He sat down, looking into the glass, twirling the ice around and around.

"I was sure sorry about what happened there at the airport, Bob," I said. "I reckon you know I wanted to stick with you."

"Yeah," he said, shortly.

"I let Conway know I didn't like it," I said.

And he said, "Yeah," again. "Forget it. Just drop it, will you?"

"Well, sure,"I nodded. "Whatever you say, Bob."

I watched him out of the corner of my eye, as I went ahead rubbing the boot. He acted mad and worried, almost disgusted you might say. But I was pretty sure it wasn't over anything I'd done. In fact, I couldn't see that Conway had done enough to upset him like this.

"Is your rheumatism bothering you again?" I said. "Why don't you face around on the straight chair where I can get at your shoulder muscles, and I'll—"

He raised his head and looked up at me. And his eyes were clear, but somehow there seemed to be tears behind them. Slowly, slowly, like he was talking to himself, he began to speak.

"I know what you are, don't I, Lou? Know you backwards and forwards. Known you since you was kneehigh to a grasshopper, and I never knowed a bad thing about you. Know just what you're goin' to say and do, no matter what you're up against. Like there at the airport— seeing Conway order me around. A lot of men in your place would have got a big bang out of that, but I knew you wouldn't. I knew you'd feel a lot more hurt about it than I did. That's the way you are, and you wouldn't know how to be any other way. . . ."

"Bob," I said. "You got something on your mind, Bob?"

"It'll keep," he said. "I reckon it'll have to keep for a while. I just wanted you to know that I—I—"

"Yes, Bob?"

"It'll keep," he repeated. "Like I said, it'll have to keep." And he clinked the ice in his glass, staring down at it. "That Howard Hendricks," he went on. "Now, Howard ought to've known better'n to put you through that foolishness this morning. 'Course, he's got his job to do, same as I got mine, and a man can't let friendship stand in the way of duty. But—"

"Oh, hell, Bob," I said. "I didn't think anything of that."

"Well, I did. I got to thinking about it this afternoon after we left the airport. I thought about how you'd have acted if you'd have been in my place and me in yours. Oh, I reckon you'd have been pleasant and friendly, because that's the way you're built. But you wouldn't have left any doubt as to where you stood. You'd have said, 'Look, now, Bob Maples is a friend of mine, and I know he's straight as a string. So if there's something we want to know, let's just up and ask him. Let's don't play no little two-bit sheepherders' tricks on him like he was on one side of the fence and we was on the other.' . . . That's what you'd have done. But me—Well, I don't know, Lou. Maybe I'm behind the times. Maybe I'm getting too old for this job."

It looked to me like he might have something there. He was getting old and unsure of himself, and Conway had probably given him a hell of a riding that I didn't know about.

"You had some trouble at the hospital, Bob?" I said.

"Yeah," he hesitated. "I had some trouble." He got up and poured more whiskey into his glass. Then, he moved over to the window and stood rocking on his heels, his back turned to me. "She's dead, Lou. She never came out of the ether."

"Well," I said. "We all knew she didn't stand a chance. Everyone but Conway, and he was just too stubborn to see reason."

He didn't say anything. I walked over to the window by him and put my arm around his shoulders.

"Look, Bob," I said. "I don't know what Conway said to you, but don't let it get you down. Where the hell does he get off at, anyway? He wasn't even going to have us come along on this trip; we had to deal ourselves in. Then, when we got back here, he wants us to jump whenever he hollers frog, and he raises hell when things don't go to suit him."

He shrugged a little, or maybe he just took a deep breath. I let my arm slide from his shoulders, hesitated a moment, thinking he was about to say something, then went into the bathroom and closed the door. When a man's feeling low, sometimes the best thing to do is leave him alone.

I sat down on the edge of the tub, and lighted a cigar. I sat thinking—standing outside of myself—thinking about myself and Bob Maples. He'd always been pretty decent to me, and I liked him. But no more, I suppose, than I liked a lot of other people. When it came right down to cases, he was just one of hundreds of people I knew and was friendly with. And yet here I was, fretting about his problems instead of my own.

Of course, that might be partly because I'd known my problems were pretty much settled. I'd known that Joyce couldn't live, that she wasn't going to talk. She might have regained consciousness for a while, but she sure as hell wouldn't have talked; not after what had happened to her face. . . . But knowing that I was safe couldn't entirely explain my concern for him. Because I'd been damned badly rattled after the murder, I hadn't been able to reason clearly, to accept the fact that I *had* to be safe. Yet I'd tried to help the Greek's boy, Johnnie Pappas.

The door slammed open, and I looked up. Bob grinned at me broadly, his face flushed, whiskey slopping to the floor from his glass.

"Hey," he said, "you runnin' out on me, Lou? Come on in here an' keep me company."

"Sure, Bob," I said. "Sure, I will." And I went back into the living room with him. He flopped down into a chair, and he drained his drink at a gulp.

"Let's do something, Lou. Let's go out and paint old cow town red. Just me'n you, huh?"

"What about Conway?"

"T'hell with him. He's got some business here; stayin' over for a few days. We'll check our bags somewheres, so's we won't have to run into him again, and then we'll have a party."

He made a grab for the bottle, and got it on the second try. I took it away from him, and filled his glass myself.

"That sounds fine, Bob," I said. "I'd sure like to do that. But shouldn't we be getting back to Central City? I mean, with Conway feeling the way he does, it might not look good for us—"

"I said t'hell with him. Said it, an' that's what I meant."

"Well, sure. But—"

"Done enough for Conway. Done too much. Done more'n any white man should. Now, c'mon and slide into them boots an' let's go."

I said, sure, sure I would. I'd do just that. But I had a bad callus, and I'd have to trim it first. So maybe, as long as he'd have to wait, he'd better lie down and take a little nap.

He did it, after a little grumbling and protesting. I called the railroad station, and reserved a bedroom on the eight o'clock train to Central City. It would cost us a few dollars personally, since the county would only pay for first-class Pullman fare. But I figured we were going to need privacy.

I was right. I woke him up at six-thirty, to give him plenty of time to get ready, and he seemed worse off than before his nap. I couldn't get him to take a bath. He wouldn't drink any coffee or eat. Instead, he started hitting the whiskey again; and when we left the hotel he took a full bottle with him. By the time I got him on the train, I was as frazzled as a cow's hide under a branding iron. I wondered what in the name of God Conway had said to him.

I wondered, and, hell, I should have known. Because he'd as good as told me. It was as plain as the nose on my face, and I'd just been too close to it to see it.

Maybe, though, it was a good thing I didn't know. For there was nothing to be done about it, nothing I could do. And I'd have been sweating blood.

Well. That was about the size of my trip to the big

town. My first trip outside the county. Straight to the hotel from the plane. Straight to the train from the hotel. Then, the long ride home at night—when there was nothing to see—closed in with a crying drunk.

Once, around midnight, a little while before he went to sleep, his mind must have wandered. For, all of a sudden, his fist wobbled out and poked me in the chest.

"Hey," I said. "Watch yourself, Bob."

"Wash—watch y'self," he mumbled. "Stop man with grin, smile worthwhile—s-stop all a' stuff spilt milk n' so on. Wha' you do that for, anyway."

"Aw," I said. "I was only kidding, Bob."

"T-tell you somethin'," he said. "T-tell you somethin' I bet you never thought of."

"Yeah?"

"It's—it's always lightest j-just before the dark."

Tired as I was, I laughed. "You got it wrong, Bob," I said. "You mean—"

"Huh-uh," he said. "You got it wrong."

10

We got into Central City around six in the morning, and Bob took a taxi straight home. He was sick; really sick, not just hung-over. He was too old a man to pack away the load he'd had.

I stopped by the office, but everything was pretty quiet, according to the night deputy, so I went on home, too. I had a lot more hours in than I'd been paid for. No one could have faulted me if I'd taken a week off. Which, naturally, I didn't intend to do.

I changed into some fresh clothes, and made some scrambled eggs and coffee. As I sat down to eat, the phone rang.

I supposed it was the office, or maybe Amy checking up on me; she'd have to call early or wait until four when her school day was over. I went to the phone, trying to think of some dodge to get out of seeing her, and when I heard Joe Rothman's voice it kind of threw me.

"Know who it is, Lou?" he said. "Remember our *late* talk."

"Sure," I said. "About the—uh—building situation."

"I'd ask you to drop around tonight, but I have to take a little jaunt to San Angelo. Would you mind if I stopped by your house a few minutes?"

"Well," I said, "I guess you could. Is it something important?"

"A small thing, but important, Lou. A matter of a few words of reassurance."

"Well, maybe I could—"

"I'm sure you could, but I think I'd better *see* you," he said; and he clicked up the receiver.

I hung up my phone, and went back to my breakfast. It was still early. The chances were that no one would see him. Anyway, he wasn't a criminal, opinion in some quarters to the contrary.

He came about five minutes later. I offered him some breakfast, not putting much warmth into the invitation since I didn't want him hanging around; and he said, no, thanks, but sat down at the table with me.

"Well, Lou," he said, starting to roll a cigarette. "I imagine you know what I want to hear."

"I think so," I nodded. "Consider it said."

"The very discreet newspaper stories are correct in their hints? He tried to dish it out and got it thrown back at him?"

"That's the way it looks. I can't think of any other explanation."

"I couldn't help wondering," he said, moistening the paper of his cigarette. "I couldn't help wondering how a woman with her face caved in and her neck broken could score six bulls-eyes on a man, even one as large as the late unlamented Elmer Conway."

He looked up slowly until his eyes met mine. I shrugged. "Probably she didn't fire all the shots at one time. She was shooting him while he was punching her. Hell, she'd hardly stand there and take it until he got through, and then start shooting."

"It doesn't seem that she would, does it?" he nodded. "Yet from the smattering of information I can gather, she must have done exactly that. She was still alive after he died; and almost any one—well, two—of the bullets she put into him was enough to lay him low. Ergo, she must have acquired the broken neck et cetera, before she did her shooting."

I shook my head. I had to get my eyes away from his.

"You said you wanted reassurance," I said. "You— you—"

"The genuine article, Lou; no substitutes accepted. And I'm still waiting to get it."

"I don't know where you get off at questioning me," I said. "The sheriff and the county attorney are satisfied. That's all I care about."

"That's the way you see it, eh?"

"That's the way I see it."

"Well, I'll tell you how I see it. I get off questioning you because I'm involved in the matter. Not directly, perhaps, but—"

"But not indirectly, either."

"Exactly. I knew you had it in for the Conways; in fact, I did everything I could to set you against the old man. Morally—perhaps even legally—I share the responsibility for any untoward action you might take. At any rate, we'll say, I and the unions I head could be placed in a very unfavorable light."

"You said it," I said. "It's your own statement."

"But don't ride that horse too hard, Lou. I don't hold still for murder. Incidentally, what's the score as of to date? One or two?"

"She's dead. She died yesterday afternoon."

"I won't buy it, Lou—if it was murder. Your doing. I can't say offhand what I will do, but I won't let you ride. I couldn't. You'd wind up getting me into something even worse."

"Oh, hell," I said. "What are we—"

"The girl's dead, and Elmer's dead. So regardless of how funny things look—and this deal should have put the courthouse crowd into hysterics—they can't prove anything. If they knew what I know, about your having a motive—"

"For killing her? Why would I want to do that?"

"Well"—he began to slow down a little—"leave her out of it. Say that she was just an instrument for getting back at Conway. A piece of stage setting."

"You know that doesn't make sense," I said. "About the other, this so-called motive—I'd had it for six years; I'd known about Mike's accident that long. Why would I wait six years, and then all of a sudden decide to pull this?

Beat some poor whore to a pulp just to get at Chester Conway's son. Now, tell me if that sounds logical. Just tell me, Joe."

Rothman frowned thoughtfully, his fingers drumming upon the table. "No," he said, slowly. "It doesn't sound logical. That's the trouble. The man who walked away from that job—if he walked away—"

"You know he didn't, Joe."

"So you say."

"So I say," I said. "So everyone says. You'd say so yourself, if you didn't know how I felt about the Conways. Put that out of your mind once, and what do you have? Why, just a double murder—two people getting in a brawl and killing each other—under kind of puzzling circumstances."

He smiled wryly. "I'd call that the understatement of the century, Lou."

"I can't tell you what happened," I said, "because I wasn't there. But I know there are flukes in murder the same as there are in anything else. A man crawls a mile with his brains blown out. A woman calls the police after she's shot through the heart. A man is hanged and poisoned and chopped up and shot, and he goes right on living. Don't ask me why those things are. I don't know. But I do know they happen, and so do you."

Rothman looked at me steadily. Then, his head jerked a little, nodding.

"I guess so, Lou," he said. "I guess you're clean, at least. I've been sitting here watching you, putting together everything I know about you, and I couldn't make it tally with the picture I've got of *that* guy. Screwy as things are, that would be even screwier. You don't fit the part, to coin a phrase."

"What do I say to that?" I said.

"Not a thing, Lou. I should be thanking you for lifting a considerable load from my mind. However, if you don't mind my going into your debt a little further . . ."

"Yes?"

"What's the lowdown, just for my own information? I'll concede that you didn't have a killing hate for Conway, but you did hate him. What are you trying to pull off?"

I'd been expecting that question since the night I'd talked to him. I had the answer all ready.

"The money was supposed to be a payoff to get her out of town. Conway was paying her to go away and leave Elmer alone. Actually—"

"—Elmer was going to leave with her, right?" Rothman got up and put on his hat. "Well, I can't find it in my heart to chide you for the stunt, despite its unfortunate outcome. I almost wish I'd thought of it."

"Aw," I said, "it wasn't nothing much. Just a matter of a will finding a way."

"Ooof!" he said. "What are Conway's feelings, by the way?"

"Well, I don't think he feels real good," I said.

"Probably something he ate," he nodded. "Don't you imagine? But watch that stuff, Lou. Watch it. Save it for those birds."

He left.

I got the newspapers out of the yard—yesterday afternoon's and this morning's—poured more coffee, and sat back down at the table.

As usual, the papers had given me all the breaks. Instead of making me look like a boob or a busybody, which they could have done easily enough, they had me down as a kind of combination J. Edgar Hoover-Lombroso, "the shrewd sheriff's sleuth whose unselfish intervention in the affair came to naught, due only to the unpredictable quirks of all-too-human behavior."

I laughed, choking on the coffee I was starting to swallow. In spite of all I'd been through, I was beginning to feel nice and relaxed. Joyce was dead. Not even Rothman suspected me. And when you passed clean with *that* guy, you didn't have anything to worry about. It was sort of an acid test, you might say.

I debated calling up the newspapers and complimenting them on their "accuracy." I often did that, spread a little sunshine, you know, and they ate it up. I could say something—I laughed—I could say something about truth being stranger than fiction. And maybe add something like—well—murder will out. Or . . . the best laid plans of mice and men.

I stopped laughing.

I was supposed to be over that stuff. Rothman had warned me about it, and it'd got Bob Maples' goat, But—

Well, why shouldn't I, if I wanted to? If it helped to take the tension out of me? It was in character. It fitted in with that dull good-natured guy who couldn't do anything bad if he tried. Rothman himself had remarked that no matter how screwy things looked, seeing me as a murderer was even screwier. And my talk was a big part of me—part of the guy that had thrown 'em all off the trail. If I suddenly stopped talking that way, what would people think?

Why, I just about had to keep on whether I wanted to or not. The choice was out of my hands. But, of course, I'd take it kind of easy. Not overdo it.

I reasoned it all out, and wound up still feeling good. But I decided not to call the newspapers, after all. The stories had been more than fair to me, but it hadn't cost 'em anything; they had to fill space some way. And I didn't care too much about a number of the details; what they said about Joyce, for example. She wasn't a "shabby sister of sin." She hadn't, for Christ's sake, "loved not wisely but too well." She was just a cute little ol' gal who'd latched onto the wrong guy, or the right guy in the wrong place; she hadn't wanted anything else, nothing else. And she'd got it. Nothing.

Amy Stanton called a little after eight o'clock, and I asked her to come over that night. The best way to stall, I figured, was not to stall; not to put any opposition to her. If I didn't hang back, she'd stop pushing me. And, after all, she couldn't get married on an hour's notice. There'd be all sorts of things to attend to, and discuss— God, how they'd have to be discussed! even the size of the douche bag to take along on our honeymoon! And long before she was through, I'd be in shape to pull out of Central City.

After I'd finished talking to her, I went into Dad's laboratory, lighted the Bunsen burner and put an intravenous needle and an ordinary hypodermic on to boil. Then, I looked along the shelves until I found a carton each of male hormone, ACTH, B-complex and sterile water. Dad's stock of drugs was getting old, of course, but the pharmaceutical houses still kept sending us samples. The samples were what I used.

I mixed up an intravenous of the ACTH, B-complex and water and put it into my right arm. (Dad had a theory that shots should never be given on the same side as the heart.) I shot the hormone into my hip . . . and I was set for the night. Amy wouldn't be disappointed again. She wouldn't have anything to wonder about. Whether my trouble had been psychosomatic or real, the result of tension or too much Joyce, I wouldn't have it tonight. Little Amy would be tamed down for a week.

I went up to my bedroom and went to sleep. I woke up at noon, when the refinery whistles began to blow; then, dozed off again and slept until after two. Sometimes, most of the time, I should say, I can sleep eighteen hours and still not feel rested. Well, I'm not tired, exactly, but I hate to get up. I just want to stay where I am, and not talk to anyone or see anyone.

Today, though, it was different; just the opposite. I could hardly wait to get cleaned up, and be out and doing something.

I showered and shaved, standing under the cold water a long time because that medicine was really working. I got into a clean tan shirt, and put on a new black bow tie, and took a freshly pressed blue suit out of the closet.

I fixed and ate a bite of lunch, and called Sheriff Maples' house.

His wife answered the phone. She said that Bob was feeling kind of poorly, and that the doctor thought he'd better stay in bed for a day or two. He was asleep, right then, and she kind of hated to wake him up. But if there was anything important . . .

"I just wondered how he was," I said. "Thought I might drop by for a few minutes."

"Well, that's mighty nice of you, Lou. I'll tell him you called when he wakes up. Maybe you can come by tomorrow if he's not up and around by then."

"Fine," I said.

I tried to read a while, but I couldn't concentrate. I wondered what to do with myself, now that I did have a day off. I couldn't shoot pool or bowl. It didn't look good for a cop to hang around pool halls and bowling alleys. It didn't look good for 'em to go into bars. It didn't look good for them to be seen in a show in the daytime.

I could drive around. Take a ride by myself. That was about all.

Gradually, the good feeling began to leave me.

I got the car out, and headed for the courthouse.

Hank Butterby, the office deputy, was reading the paper, his boots up on the desk, his jaws moving on a cud of tobacco. He asked me if it was hot enough for me, and why'n hell I didn't stay home when I had a chance. I said, well, you know how it is, Hank.

"Nice goin'," he said, nodding at the paper. "Right

pretty little piece they got about you. I was just fixin' to clip it out and save it for you."

The stupid son-of-a-bitch was always doing that. Not just stories about me, but everything. He'd clip out cartoons and weather reports and crappy poems and health columns. Every goddam thing under the sun. He couldn't read a paper without a pair of scissors.

"I'll tell you what," I said, "I'll autograph it for you, and you keep it. Maybe it'll be valuable some day."

"Well"—he slanted his eyes at me, and looked quickly away again—"I wouldn't want to put you to no trouble, Lou."

"No trouble at all," I said. "Here let me have it," I scrawled my name along the margin, and handed it back to him. "Just don't let this get around," I said. "If I have to do the same thing for the other fellows, it'll run the value down."

He stared at the paper, glassy-eyed, like maybe it was going to bite him. "Uh"—there it went; he'd forgot and swallowed his spit—"you really think . . . ?"

"Here's what you do," I said, getting my elbows down on the desk and whispering. "Go out to one of the refineries, and get 'em to steam you out a steel drum. Then—you know anyone that'll lend you a welding torch?"

"Yeah"—he was whispering too. "I think I can borry one."

"Well, cut the drum in two, cut it around twice, rather, so's you'll have kind of a lid. Then put that autographed clipping inside—the only one in existence, Hank!—and weld it back together again. Sixty or seventy years from now, you can take it to some museum and they'll pay you a fortune for it."

"Cripes!" he said. "You keepin' a drum like that, Lou? Want me to pick you up one?"

"Oh, I guess not," I said. "I probably won't live that long."

11

I hesitated in the corridor in front of Howard Hendricks' office, and he glanced up from his desk and waved to me.

"Hello, there, Lou. Come on in and sit a minute."

I went in, nodding to his secretary, and pulled a chair up to the desk. "Just talked to Bob's wife a little while ago," I said. "He's not feeling so good."

"So I hear." He struck a match for my cigar. "Well, it doesn't matter much. I mean there's nothing more to be done on this Conway case. All we can do is sit tight; just be available in the event that Conway starts tossing his weight around. I imagine he'll become resigned to the situation before too long."

"It was too bad about the girl dying," I said.

"Oh, I don't know, Lou," he shrugged. "I can't see that she'd have been able to tell us anything we don't already know. Frankly, and just between the two of us, I'm rather relieved. Conway wouldn't have been satisfied unless she went to the chair with all the blame pinned on her. I'd have hated to be a party to it."

"Yeah," I said. "That wouldn't have been so good."

"Though of course I would have, Lou, if she'd lived. I mean, I'd have prosecuted her to the hilt."

He was leaning backwards to be friendly since our brush the day before. I was his old pal, and he was letting me know his innermost feelings.

"I wonder, Howard . . ."

"Yes, Lou?"

"Well, I guess I'd better not say it," I said. "Maybe you don't feel like I do about things."

"Oh, I'm sure I do. I've always felt we had a great deal in common. What is it you wanted to tell me?"

His eyes strayed a second from mine, and his mouth quirked a little. I knew his secretary had winked at him.

"Well, it's like this," I said. "Now, I've always felt we were one big happy family here. Us people that work for the county . . ."

"Uh-huh. One big happy family, eh?" His eyes strayed again. "Go on, Lou."

"We're kind of brothers under the skin. . . ."

"Y-yes."

"We're all in the same boat, and we've got to put our shoulders to the wheel and pull together."

His throat seemed to swell all of a sudden, and he yanked a handkerchief from his pocket. Then he whirled around in his chair, his back to me, coughing and strangling and sputtering. I heard his secretary get up, and hurry out. Her high heels went tap-tapping down the corridor, moving faster and faster toward the woman's john until she was almost running.

I hoped she pissed in her drawers.

I hoped that chunk of shrapnel under his ribs had punctured a lung. That chunk of shrapnel had cost the taxpayers a hell of a pile of dough. He'd got elected to office talking about that shrapnel. Not cleaning up the county and seeing that everyone got a fair shake. Just shrapnel.

He finally straightened up and turned around, and I told him he'd better take care of that cold. "I'll tell you what I always do," I said. "I take the water from a boiled onion, and squeeze a big lemon into it. Well, maybe a middling-size lemon and a small one if—"

"Lou!" he said sharply.

"Yeah?" I said.

"I appreciate your sentiments—your interest—but I'll have to ask you to come to the point. What did you wish to tell me, anyway?"

"Oh, it wasn't any—"

"Please, Lou!"

"Well, here's what I was wondering about," I said. And I told him. The same thing that Rothman had wondered about. I put it into my words, drawling it out, slow and awkward. That would give him something to worry over. Something besides flat-tire tracks. And the beauty of it was he couldn't do much but worry.

"Jesus," he said, slowly. "It's right there, isn't it? Right out in the open, when you look at it right. It's one of those things that are so plain and simple you don't see 'em. No matter how you turn it around, he just about had to kill her after he was dead. After he couldn't do it!"

"Or vice versa," I said.

He wiped his forehead, excited but kind of sick-looking.

Trying to trap old simple Lou with the tire tracks was one thing. That was about his speed. But this had him thrown for a loop.

"You know what this means, Lou?"

"Well, it doesn't necessarily mean that," I said, and I gave him an out. I rehashed the business about fluke deaths that I'd given to Rothman. "That's probably the way it was. Just one of those damned funny things that no one can explain."

"Yeah," he said. "Of course. That's bound to be it. You—uh—you haven't mentioned this to anyone, Lou?"

I shook my head. "Just popped into my mind a little while ago. 'Course, if Conway's still riled up when he gets back, I—"

"I don't believe I would, Lou. I really don't think that'd be wise, at all."

"You mean I should tell Bob, first? Oh, I intended to do that. I wouldn't go over Bob's head."

"No, Lou," he said, "that isn't what I mean. Bob isn't well. He's already taken an awful pounding from Conway. I don't think we should trouble him with anything else. Something which, as you point out, is doubtless of no consequence."

"Well," I said, "if it doesn't amount to anything, I don't see why—"

"Let's just keep it to ourselves, Lou, for the time being, at least. Just sit tight and see what happens. After all, what else can we do? What have we got to go on?"

"Nothing much," I said. "Probably nothing at all."

"Exactly! I couldn't have stated it better."

"I tell you what we might do," I said. "It wouldn't be too hard to round up all the men that visited her. Probably ain't more than thirty or forty of 'em, her being a kind of high-priced gal. Bob and us, our crowd, we could round 'em up, and you could . . ."

I wish you could have seen him sweat. Rounding up thirty or forty well-to-do citizens wouldn't be any skin off our ass, the sheriff's office. He'd be the one to study the evidence, and ask for indictments. By the time he was through, he'd be *through*. He couldn't be elected dogcatcher, if shrapnel was running out of his eyeballs.

Well, though, I didn't really want him to do it any more than he wanted to. The case was closed, right on Elmer Conway's neck, and it was a darned good idea to leave it that way. So, that being the case, and seeing it was about supper time, I allowed him to convince me. I said I didn't have much sense about such things, and I was sure grateful for his setting me straight. And that's the way it ended. Almost.

I gave him my recipe for curing coughs before I left.

I sauntered down to my car, whistling; thinking of what a fine afternoon it had been, after all, and what a hell of a kick there'd be in talking about it.

Ten minutes later I was out on Derrick Road, making a U-turn back toward town.

I don't know why. Well, I do know. She was the only person I could have talked to, who'd have understood what I was talking about. But I knew she wasn't there. I knew she'd never be there again, there or anywhere. She was gone and I knew it. So . . . I don't know why.

I drove back toward town, back toward the rambling old two-story house and the barn where the rats squealed. And once I said, "I'm sorry, baby." I said it out loud. "You'll never know how sorry I am." Then I said, "You understand, don't you? In a few months more I couldn't have stopped. I'd have lost all control and . . ."

A butterfly struck lightly against the wind-screen, and fluttered away again. I went back to my whistling.

It had sure been a fine afternoon.

I was about out of groceries, so I stopped at a grocery and picked up a few, including a steak for my dinner. I went home and fixed myself a whopping big meal, and ate every bite of it. That B-complex was really doing its job. So was the other stuff. I began to actually look forward to seeing Amy. I began to want her bad.

I washed and wiped the dishes. I mopped the kitchen floor, dragging the job out as long as I could. I wrung the mop out and hung it up on the back porch, and came back and looked at the clock. The hands seemed to have been standing still. It would be at least a couple of hours yet before she'd dare to come over.

There wasn't any more work I could do, so I filled a big cup with coffee and took it up into Dad's office. I set it on his desk, lighted a cigar and started browsing along the rows of books.

Dad always said that he had enough trouble sorting the fiction out of so-called facts, without reading fiction. He always said that science was already too muddled without trying to make it jibe with religion. He said those things, but he also said that science in itself could be a religion, that a broad mind was always in danger of becoming narrow. So there was quite a bit of fiction on the shelves, and as much Biblical literature, probably, as a lot of ministers had.

I'd read some of the fiction. The other I'd left alone. I went to church and Sunday school, living as I had to live, but that was the end of it. Because kids are kids; and if that sounds pretty obvious, all I can say is that a lot of supposedly deep thinkers have never discovered the fact. A kid hears you cussing all the time, and he's going to cuss, too. He won't understand if you tell him it's wrong. He's loyal, and if you do it, it must be all right.

As I say, then, I'd never looked into any of the religious literature around the house. But I did tonight. I'd already read almost everything else. And I think it was in my mind that, since I was going to sell this place, I'd better be checking things over for value.

So I reached down a big leather-bound concordance to the Bible and blew the dust off of it. And I carried it over to the desk and opened it up; it kind of slid open by itself when I laid it down. And there was a picture in it, a little two-by-four snapshot, and I picked it up.

I turned it around one way, then another. I turned it sideways and upside down—what I thought was upside down. And I kind of grinned like a man will, when he's interested and puzzled.

It was a woman's face, not pretty exactly, but the kind that gets to you without your knowing why. But where the hell it was, what she was doing, I couldn't make out. Offhand, it looked like she was peering through the crotch of a tree, a white maple, say, with two limbs tapering up from the bole. She had her hands clasped around the limbs, and . . . But I knew that couldn't be right. Because the bole was divided at the base, and there were stumps of chopped off limbs almost tangent to the others.

I rubbed the picture against my shirt, and looked at it again. That face was familiar. It was coming back to me from some faraway place, like something coming out of hiding. But it was old, the picture I mean, and there were kind of crisscross blurs—of age, I supposed—scarring whatever she was looking through.

I took a magnifying glass and looked at it. I turned it upside down, as it was supposed to be turned. Then, I kind of dropped the glass and shoved it away from me; and I sat staring into space. At nothing and everything.

She was looking through a crotch, all right. But it was her own.

She was on her knees, peering between them. And those crisscross blurs on her thighs weren't the result of age. They were scars. The woman was Helene, who had been Dad's housekeeper so long ago.

Dad . . .

12

I was only like that for a few minutes, sitting there and staring, but a world of things, most of my kid life, came back to me in that time. *She* came back to me, the house-keeper, and she had been so much of that life.

"Want to fight, Helene? Want to learn how to box . . . ?"
And:
"Oh, I'm tired. You just hit me. . . ."
And:
"But you'll like it, darling. All the big boys do it. . . ."
I lived back through it all, and then I came to the end of it. That last terrible day, with me crouched at the foot of the stairs, sick with fear and shame, terrified, aching with the first and only whipping in my life; listening to the low angry voices, the angry and contemptuous voices, in the library.

"I am not arguing with you, Helene. You're leaving here tonight. Consider yourself lucky that I don't prosecute you."

"Oh, ye-ss? I'd like to see you try it!"

"Why, Helene? How in the world could you do such a thing?"

"Jealous?"

"You—a mere child, and—"

"Yes! That's right! A mere child. Why not remember that? Listen to me, Daniel. I—"

"Don't say it, please. I'm at fault. If I hadn't—"

"Has it hurt you any? Have you harmed anyone? Haven't you, in fact—I should ask!—gradually lost all interest in it?"

"But a child! My child. My only son. If anything should happen—"

"Uh-huh. That's what bothers you, isn't it? Not him, but you. How it would reflect on you."

"Get out! A woman with no more sensibilities than—"

"I'm white trash, that's the term, isn't it? Riffraff. I ain't got that ol' quality. All right, and when I see some hypocritical son-of-a-bitch like you, I'm damned glad of it!"

"Get out or I'll kill you!"

"Tsk-tsk! But think of the disgrace, Doctor . . . Now, I'm going to tell you something. . . ."

"Get—"

"Something that you above all people should know. This didn't need to mean a thing. Absolutely nothing. But now it will. You've handled it in the worst possible way. You—"

"I . . . please, Helene."

"You'll never kill anyone. Not you. You're too damned smug and self-satisfied and sure of yourself. You like to hurt people, but—"

"No!"

"All right. I'm wrong. You're the great, good Dr. Ford, and I'm white trash, so that makes me wrong . . . I hope."

That was all.

I'd forgotten about it, and now I forgot it again. There are things that have to be forgotten if you want to go on living. And somehow I did want to; I wanted to more than ever. If the Good Lord made a mistake in us people it was in making us want to live when we've got the least excuse for it.

I put the concordance back on the shelf. I took the picture into the laboratory and burned it, and washed the ashes down the sink. But it was a long time burning, it seemed like. And I couldn't help noticing something:

How much she looked like Joyce. How there was even a strong resemblance between her and Amy Stanton.

The phone rang. I wiped my hands against my pants, and answered it, looking at myself in the laboratory door mirror—at the guy in the black bow tie and the pink-tan shirt, his trouser legs hooked over his boot tops.

"Lou Ford, speakin'," I said.

"Howard, Lou. Howard Hendricks. Look. I want you to come right down . . . down to the courthouse, yeah."

"Well, I don't know about that," I said. "I kind of—"

"She'll have to wait, Lou. This is important!" It had to be, the way he was sputtering. "Remember what we were talking about this afternoon? About the—you know—the possibility of an outside party being the murderer. Well, you, we were dead right. Our hunch was right!"

"Huh!" I said. "But it couldn't—I mean—"

"We've got him, Lou! We've got the son-of-a-bitch! We've got the bastard cold, and—"

"You mean he's admitted it? Hell, Howard, there's always some crank confessing to—"

"He's not admitting anything! He won't even talk! That's why we need you. We can't, uh, work on him, you know, but you can make him talk. You can soften him up if anyone can. I think you know him, incidentally."

"W-who-yeah?"

"The Greek's kid, Johnnie Pappas. You know him; he's been in plenty of trouble before. Now, get down here, Lou. I've already called Chester Conway and he's flying out from Fort Worth in the morning. I gave you full credit—told him how we'd worked on this idea together and we'd been sure all along that Elmer wasn't guilty, and . . . and he's pleased as punch, Lou. Boy, if we can just crack this, get a confession right—"

"I'll come down," I said. "I'll be right down, Howard."

I lowered the receiver hook for a moment, figuring out what had happened, what must have happened. Then, I called Amy.

Her folks were still up so she couldn't talk much; and that was a help. I made her understand that I really wanted to see her—and I did—and I shouldn't be gone too long.

I hung up and took out my wallet, and spread all the bills out on the desk.

I hadn't had any twenties of my own, just the twenty-five Elmer'd given me. And when I saw that five of them were gone, I went limp clear down to my toenails. Then I remembered that I'd used four in Forth Worth on my railroad ticket, and that I'd only broken one here in town where it would matter. Only the one . . . with Johnnie Pappas. So . . .

So I got out the car, and drove down to the courthouse.

Office Deputy Hank Butterby gave me a hurt look, and another deputy that was there, Jeff Plummer, winked and said howdy to me. Then Howard bustled in and grabbed me by the elbow, and hustled me into his office.

"What a break, huh, Lou?" He was almost slobbering with excitement. "Now, I'll tell you how to handle it. Here's what you'd better do. Sweet talk him, know what I mean, and get his guard down; then tighten up on him. Tell him if he'll cooperate we'll get him off with manslaughter—we can't do it, of course, but what you say won't be binding on me. Otherwise, tell him, it'll be the chair. He's eighteen years old, past eighteen, and—"

I stared at him. He misread my look.

"Oh, hell," he said, jabbing me in the ribs with his thumb. "Who am I to be telling you what to do? Don't I know how you handle these guys? Haven't I—"

"You haven't told me anything yet," I said. "I know Johnnie's kind of wild, but I can't see him as a murderer. What are you supposed to have on him?"

"Supposed, hell! We've got"—he hesitated—"well, here's the situation, Lou. Elmer took ten thousand bucks out there to that chippy's house. He was supposed to have taken that much. But when we counted it up, five hundred dollars was missing. . . ."

"Yeah?" I said. It was like I'd figured. That damned Elmer hadn't wanted to admit that he didn't have any dough of his own.

"Well, we thought, Bob and I did, that Elmer had probably pissed it off in a crap game or something like that. But the bills were all marked, see, and the old man had already tipped off the local banks. If she tried to hang around town after the payoff, he was going to crack down on her for blackmail. . . . That Conway! They don't put many past him!"

"It looks like they've put a few past me." I said.

"Now, Lou"—he clapped me on the back. "There's no reason to feel that way at all. We trusted you implicitly. But it was Conway's show, and—well, you *were* there in the vicinity, Lou, and . . ."

"Let it go," I said. "Johnnie spent some of the money?"

"A twenty. He broke it at a drugstore last night and it went to the bank this morning, and it was traced back to him a couple hours ago when we picked him up. Now—"

"How do you know Elmer didn't blow in the dough, and it's just now beginning to circulate?"

"None of it's shown up. Just this one twenty. So—Wait, Lou. Wait just a minute. Let me give you the whole picture, and we'll save time. I was entirely willing to concede that he'd come by the money innocently. He pays himself there at the filling station, and oddly enough that pay comes to exactly twenty dollars for the two nights. It looked all right, see what I mean? He could have taken the twenty in and paid himself with it. But he couldn't say he did—wouldn't say anything—because he damned well couldn't. There's damned few cars stopping at Murphy's between midnight and eight o'clock. He'd have to remember anyone that gave him a twenty. We could have checked the customer or customers, and he'd have been out of here—*if* he was innocent."

"Maybe it was in his cash drawer at the start of his shift?"

"Are you kidding? A twenty-dollar bill to make change with?" Hendricks shook his head. "We'd know he didn't have it, even without Slim Murphy's word. Now, wait! Hold up! We've checked on Murphy, and his alibi's airtight. The kid—huh-uh. From about nine Sunday night until eleven, his time can't be accounted for. We can't account for it, and he won't. . . . Oh, it's a cinch, Lou, anyway you look at it. Take the murders themselves— that dame beaten to a pulp. That's something a crazy kid would lose his head and do. And the money; only five hundred taken out of ten grand. He's overwhelmed by so much dough, so he grabs up a fistful and leaves the rest. A kid stunt again."

"Yeah," I said. "Yeah, I guess you're right, Howard. You think he's got the rest cached somewhere?"

"Either that or he's got scared and thrown it away. He's a set-up, Lou. Man, I've never seen one so pretty. If he dropped dead right now I'd consider it a judgment from heaven, and I'm not a religious man either!"

Well, he'd said it all. He'd proved it in black and white.

"Well, you'd better get busy, now, Lou. We've got him on ice. Haven't booked him yet, and we're not going to until he comes through. I'm not letting some shyster tell him about his rights at this stage of the game."

I hesitated. Then I said, "No, I don't reckon that would be so smart. There's nothing to be gained by that . . . Does Bob know about this?"

"Why bother him? There's nothing he can do."

"Well, I just wondered if we should ask him—if it would be all right for me to—"

"Be all right?" He frowned. "Why wouldn't it be all right? . . . Oh, I know how you feel, Lou. He's just a kid; you know him. But he's a murderer, Lou, and a damned cold-blooded one. Keep that in your mind. Think of how that poor damned woman must have felt while he was beating her face in. You saw her. You saw what her face looked like. Stew meat, hamburger—"

"Don't," I said. "For Christ's sake!"

"Sure, Lou, sure." He dropped an arm around my shoulders. "I'm sorry. I keep forgetting that you've never become hardened to this stuff. Well?"

"Well," I said. "I guess I'd better get it over with."

I walked downstairs to the basement, the jail. The turnkey let me through the gate and closed it again; and we went down past the bullpen and the regular cells to a heavy steel door. There was a small port or peephole in it, and I peered through it. But I couldn't see anything. You couldn't keep a light globe in the place, no matter what kind of guard you put over it;

and the basement window, which was two-thirds below the surface of the ground, didn't let in much natural light.

"Want to borrow a flash, Lou?"

"I guess not," I said. "I can see all I need to."

He opened the door a few inches, and I slid inside, and he slammed it behind me. I stood with my back to it a moment, blinking, and there was a squeak and a scrape, and a shadow rose up and faltered toward me.

He fell into my arms, and I held him there, patting him on the back, comforting him.

"It's all right, Johnnie boy. Everything's going to be all right."

"J-jesus, Lou. Jesus Jesus Ca-Christ. I knew—I kn-new you'd come, they'd send for you. But it was so long, so long and I began to think maybe—maybe—you'd—"

"You know me better'n that, Johnnie. You know how much I think of you."

"S-sure." He drew a long breath, and let it out slowly; like a man that's made land after a hard swim. "You got a cigarette, Lou? These dirty bastards took all my—"

"Now, now," I said. "They were just doing their duty, Johnnie. Have a cigar and I'll smoke one with you."

We sat down side by side on the bolted-down bunk, and I held a match for our cigars. I shook the match out, and he puffed and I puffed, and the glow came and went from our faces.

"This is going to burn the old man up." He laughed jerkily. "I guess—He'll have to know, won't he?"

"Yes," I said. "I'm afraid he'll have to know, Johnnie."

"How soon can I leave?"

"Very soon. It won't be long now," I said. "Where were you Sunday night?"

"To a picture show." He drew hard on his cigar, and I could see his jaw beginning to set. "What's the difference?"

"You know what I mean, Johnnie. Where'd you go after the show—between the time you left it and started to work?"

"Well"—*puff, puff*—"I don't see what that's got to do with this. I don't ask you"—*puff*—"where you—"

"You can," I said. "I intend to tell you. I guess maybe you don't know me as well as I thought you did, Johnnie. Haven't I always shot square with you?"

"Aw, hell, Lou," he said, shamed. "You know how I feel about you, but—All right, I'd probably tell you sooner or later anyway. It was"—*puff*—"here's the way it was, Lou. I told the old man I had this hot date Wednesday, see, but I was afraid of my tires, and I could pick up a couple good ones cheap an' hand him back something each week until I got 'em paid for. And—"

"Let me sort that out," I said. "You needed tires for your hot rod and you tried to borrow the money from your father?"

"Sure! Just like I said. And you know what he says, Lou? He tells me I don't need tires, that I gad around too much. He says I should bring this babe to the house and Mom'll make some ice cream, an' we'll all play cards or somethin'! For Christ's sake!" He shook his head bewilderedly. "How stupid can a person get?"

I laughed gently. "You got your two tires anyway, then?" I said. "You stripped a couple off a parked car?"

"Well—uh—to tell the truth, Lou, I took four. I wasn't meaning to but I knew where I could turn a couple real quick, an'—well—"

"Sure," I said. "This gal was kind of hard to get, and you wanted to be sure of getting over with her. A really hot babe, huh?"

"Mmmmph-umph! Wow! You know what I mean, Lou. One of those gals that makes you want to take your shoes off and wade around in her."

I laughed again, and he laughed. Then it was somehow awfully silent, and he shifted uneasily.

"I know who owned the car, Lou. Soon as I get squared away a little I'll send him the money for those tires."

"That's all right," I said. "Don't worry about it."

"Are we—uh—can I—?"

"In just a little," I said. "You'll be leaving in a few minutes, Johnnie. Just a few formalities to take care of first."

"Boy, will I be glad to be out of here! Gosh, Lou, I don't know how people stand it! It'd drive me crazy."

"It'd drive anyone crazy," I said. "It does drive them crazy . . . Maybe you'd better lie down a while, Johnnie. Stretch out on the bunk, I've got a little more talking to do."

"But"—he turned slowly and tried to look at me, to see my face.

"You'd better do that," I said. "The air gets kind of bad with both of us sitting up."

"Oh," he said. "Yeah." And he lay down. He sighed deeply. "Say, this feels pretty good. Ain't it funny, Lou, what a difference it makes? Having someone to talk to, I mean. Someone that likes you and understands you. If you've got that, you can put up with almost anything."

"Yes," I said. "It makes a lot of difference, and—That's that. You didn't tell 'em you got that twenty from me, Johnnie?"

"Hell, no! What do you think I am, anyway? Piss on those guys."

"Why not?" I said. "Why didn't you tell them?"

"Well, uh"—the hard boards of the bunk squeaked— "well, I figured—oh, you know, Lou. Elmer got around in some kind of funny places, an' I thought maybe—well, I know you don't make a hell of a lot of dough, and you're always tossing it around on other people—and if someone should slip you a little tip—"

"I see," I said. "I don't take bribes, Johnnie."

"Who said anything about bribes?" I could feel him shrug. "Who said anything? I just wasn't going to let 'em hit you cold with it until you figured out a—until you remembered where you found it."

I didn't say anything for a minute. I just sat there thinking about him, this kid that everyone said was no good, and a few other people I knew. Finally I said, "I wish you hadn't done it, Johnnie. It was the wrong thing to do."

"You mean they'll be sore?" He grunted. "To hell with

'em. They don't mean anything to me, but you're a square joe."

"Am I?" I said. "How do you know I am, Johnnie? How can a man ever really know anything? We're living in a funny world, kid, a peculiar civilization. The police are playing crooks in it, and the crooks are doing police duty. The politicians are preachers, and the preachers are politicians. The tax collectors collect for themselves. The Bad People want us to have more dough, and the Good People are fighting to keep it from us. It's not good for us, know what I mean? If we all had all we wanted to eat, we'd crap too much. We'd have inflation in the toilet paper industry. That's the way I understand it. That's about the size of some of the arguments I've heard."

He chuckled and dropped his cigar butt to the floor. "Gosh, Lou. I sure enjoy hearing you talk—I've never heard you talk that way before—but it's getting kind of late and—"

"Yeah, Johnnie," I said, "it's a screwed up, bitched up world, and I'm afraid it's going to stay that way. And I'll tell you why. Because no one, almost no one, sees anything wrong with it. They can't see that things are screwed up, so they're not worried about it. What they're worried about is guys like you.

"They're worried about guys liking a drink and taking it. Guys getting a piece of tail without paying a preacher for it. Guys who know what makes 'em feel good, and aren't going to be talked out of the motion . . . They don't like you guys, and they crack down on you. And the way it looks to me they're going to be cracking down harder and harder as time goes on. You ask me why I stick around, knowing the score, and it's hard to explain. I guess I kind of got a foot on both fences, Johnnie. I planted 'em there early and now they've taken root, and I can't move either way and I can't jump. All I can do is wait until I split. Right down the middle. That's all I can do and . . . But, you, Johnnie. Well, maybe you did the right thing. Maybe it's best this way. Because it would get harder all the time, kid, and I know how hard it's been in the past."

"I . . . I don't—"

"I killed her, Johnnie. I killed both of them. And don't say I couldn't have, that I'm not that kind of a guy, because you don't know."

"I"—He started to rise up on his elbow, then lay back again. "I'll bet you had a good reason, Lou. I bet they had it coming."

"No one has it coming to them," I said. "But I had a reason, yes."

Dimly in the distance, like a ghost hooting, I heard the refinery whistles blowing for the swing shifts. And I could picture the workmen plodding in to their jobs, and the other shifts plodding out. Tossing their lunch buckets into their cars. Driving home and playing with their kids and drinking beer and watching their television sets and diddling their wives and . . . Just as if nothing was happening. Just as if a kid wasn't dying and a man, part of a man, dying with him.

"Lou . . ."

"Yes, Johnnie." It was a statement, not a question.

"Y-you m-mean I—I should take the rap for you? I—"

"No," I said. "Yes."

"I d-d-don't think—I can't, Lou! Oh, Jesus, I can't! I c-couldn't go through—"

I eased him back on the bunk. I ruffled his hair, chucked him gently under the chin, tilting it back.

" 'There is a time of peace,' " I said, " 'and a time of war. A time to sow and a time to reap. A time to live and a time to die . . .' "

"L-Lou . . ."

"This hurts me," I said, "worse than it does you."

And I knifed my hand across his windpipe. Then I reached down for his belt.

. . . I pounded on the door, and after a minute the turnkey came. He cracked the door open a little and I slid out, and he slammed it again.

"Give you any trouble, Lou?"

"No," I said, "he was real peaceful. I think we've broken the case."

"He's gonna talk, huh?"

"They've talked before," I shrugged.

I went back upstairs and told Howard Hendricks I'd had a long talk with Johnnie, and that I thought he'd come through all right. "Just leave him alone for an hour or so," I said. "I've done everything I can. If I haven't made him see the light, then he just ain't going to see it."

"Certainly, Lou, certainly. I know your reputation. You want me to call you after I see him?"

"I wish you would," I said. "I'm kind of curious to know if he talks."

13

I've loafed around the streets sometimes, leaned against a store front with my hat pushed back and one boot hooked back around the other—hell, you've probably seen me if you've ever been out this way—I've stood like that, looking nice and friendly and stupid, like I wouldn't piss if my pants were on fire. And all the time I'm laughing myself sick inside. Just watching the people.

You know what I mean—the couples, the men and wives you see walking along together. The tall fat women, and the short scrawny men. The teensy little women, and the big fat guys. The dames with lantern jaws, and the men with no chins. The bowlegged wonders, and the knock-kneed miracles. The . . . I've laughed—inside, that is—until my guts ached. It's almost as good as dropping in on a Chamber of Commerce luncheon where some guy gets up and clears his throat a few times and says, "Gentlemen, we can't expect to get any more out of life than what we put into it . . ." (Where's the percentage in that?) And I guess it—they—the people—those mismatched peo-

ple—aren't something to laugh about. They're really trag-
ical.

They're not stupid, no more than average anyway.
They've not tied up together just to give jokers like me a
bang. The truth is, I reckon, that life has played a hell of
a trick on 'em. There was a time, just for a few minutes
maybe, when all their differences seemed to vanish and
they were just what each other wanted; when they looked
at each other at exactly the right time in the right place
and under the right circumstances. And everything was
perfect. They had that time—those few minutes—and they
never had any other. But while it lasted . . .

. . . Everything seemed the same as usual. The shades
were drawn, and the bathroom door was open a little,
just to let in a little light; and she was sprawled out on
her stomach asleep. Everything was the same . . . but it
wasn't. It was one of those times.

She woke up while I was undressing; some change
dropped out of my pocket and rolled against the base-
board. She sat up, rubbing at her eyes, starting to say
something sharp. But somehow she smiled, instead, and I
smiled back at her. I scooped her up in my arms and sat
down on the bed and held her. I kissed her, and her mouth
opened a little, and her arms locked around my neck.

That's the way it started. That's the way it went.

Until, finally, we were stretched out close, side by side,
her arm around my hips and mine around hers; limp,
drained dry, almost breathless. And still we wanted each

other—wanted something. It was like the beginning instead of the end.

She burrowed her head against my shoulder, and it was nice. I didn't feel like shoving her away. She whispered into my ear, kind of baby-talking.

"Mad at you. You hurt me."

"I did?" I said. "Gosh, I'm sorry, honey."

"Hurt real bad. 'Iss one. Punch elbow in it."

"Well, gosh—"

She kissed me, let her mouth slide off mine. "Not mad," she whispered.

She was silent then, waiting, it seemed, for me to say something. Do something. She pushed closer, squirming, still keeping her face hidden.

"Bet I know something . . ."

"Yeah, honey?"

"About that vas—that operation."

"What," I said, "do you think you know?"

"It was after that—after Mike—"

"What about Mike?"

"Darling"—she kissed my shoulder—"I don't care. I don't mind. But it was then, wasn't it? Your father got ex—worried and . . . ?"

I let my breath out slowly. Almost any other night I could have enjoyed wringing her neck, but this was one time when I hadn't felt that way.

"It was about that time, as I recollect," I said. "But I don't know as that had anything to do with it."

"Honey . . ."

"Yeah?"

"Why do you suppose people . . . ?"

"It beats me," I said. "I never have been able to figure it out."

"D-don't some women . . . I'll bet you would think it was awful if—"

"If what?"

She pushed against me, and it felt like she was on fire. She shivered and began to cry. "D-don't, Lou. Don't make me ask. J-just . . ."

So I didn't make her ask.

Later on, when she was still crying but in a different way, the phone rang. It was Howard Hendricks.

"Lou, kid, you really did it! You really softened him up!"

"He signed a confession?" I said.

"Better than that, boy! He hanged himself! Did it with his belt! That proves he was guilty without us having to screw around before a judge and put the taxpayers to a lot of expense, and all that crap! Goddammit, Lou, I wish I was there right now to shake your hand!"

He stopped yelling and tried to get the gloat out of his voice. "Now, Lou, I want you to promise me that you won't take this the wrong way. You mustn't get down about it. A person like that don't deserve to live. He's a lot better off dead than he is alive."

"Yeah," I said. "I guess you're right at that."

I got rid of him and hung up. And right away the phone rang again. This time it was Chester Conway calling from Fort Worth.

"Great work, Lou. Fine job. Fine! Guess you know what this means to me. Guess I made a mistake about—"

"Yes?" I said.

"Nothing. Don't matter now . . . See you, boy."

I hung up again, and the phone rang a third time. Bob Maples. His voice came over the wire thin and shaky.

"I know how much you thought of that boy, Lou. I know you'd just about as soon it'd happened to yourself."

As soon? "Yeah, Bob," I said. "I just about would have."

"You want to come over and set a spell, Lou? Play a game of checkers or somethin'? I ain't supposed to be up or I'd offer to come over there."

"I—I reckon not, Bob," I said. "But thanks, thanks a heap."

"That's all right, son. You change your mind, come on over. No matter what time it is."

Amy'd been taking in everything; impatient, curious. I hung up and slumped down on the bed, and she sat up beside me.

"For heaven's sake! What was that all about, Lou?"

I told her. Not the truth, of course, but what was supposed to be the truth. She clapped her hands together.

"Oh, darling! That's wonderful. My Lou solving the case! . . . Will you get a reward?"

"Why should I?" I said. "Think of all the fun I had."

"Oh, well . . ." She drew away a little, and I thought she was going to pop off; and I reckon she wanted to. But she wanted something else worse. "I'm sorry, Lou. You have every right to be angry with me."

She lay back down again, turning on her stomach, spreading her arms and legs. She stretched out, waiting, and whispered:

"Very, very angry . . ."

Sure, I know. Tell me something else. Tell a hophead he shouldn't take dope. Tell him it'll kill him, and see if he stops.

She got her money's worth.

It was going to cost her plenty, and I gave her value received. Honest Lou, that was me, Let Lou Titillate Your Tail.

14

I guess I must have got to sweating with all that exercise, and not having any clothes on I caught a hell of a cold. Oh, it wasn't too bad; not enough to really lay me low; but I wasn't fit to do any chasing around. I had to stay in bed for a week. And it was kind of a break for me, you might say.

I didn't have to talk to a lot of people, and have 'em asking damned fool questions and slapping me on the back. I didn't have to go to Johnnie Pappas' funeral. I didn't have to call on his folks, like I'd have felt I had to do ordinarily.

A couple of the boys from the office dropped by to say hello, and Bob Maples came in a time or two. He was still looking very pretty peaked, seemed to have aged about ten years. We kept off the subject of Johnnie—just talked about things in general—and the visits went off pretty well. Only one thing came up that kind of worried me for a while. It was on the first—no, I guess the second time he came by.

"Lou," he said, "why in hell don't you get out of this town?"

"Get out?" I was startled. We'd just been sitting there quietly, smoking and passing a word now and then. And suddenly he comes out with this. "Why should I get out?"

"Why've you ever stayed here this long?" he said. "Why'd you ever want to wear a badge? Why didn't you be a doctor like your dad; try to make something of yourself?"

I shook my head, staring down at the bedclothes. "I don't know, Bob. Reckon I'm kind of lazy."

"You got awful funny ways of showin' it, Lou. You ain't never too lazy to take on some extra job. You put in more hours than any man I got. An' if I know anything about you, you don't like the work. You never have liked it."

He wasn't exactly right about that, but I knew what he meant. There was other work I'd have liked a lot better. "I don't know, Bob," I said, "there's a couple of kinds of laziness. The don't-want-to-do-nothin' and the stick-in-the-rut brand. You take a job, figuring you'll just keep it a little while, and that while keeps stretchin' on and on and on. You need a little more money before you can make a jump. You can't quite make up your mind about what you want to jump to. And then maybe you make a stab at it, you send off a few letters, and the people want to know what experience you've had—what you've been doin'. And probably they don't even want to bother with you, and if they do you've got to start right at the bottom, because you don't know anything. So you stay where you

are, you just about got to, and you work pretty hard because you know it. You ain't young anymore and it's all
you've got."

Bob nodded slowly. "Yeah . . . I kinda know how that
is. But it didn't need to be that way with you, Lou! Your
dad could've sent you off to school. You could've been a
practicin' doctor by this time."

"Well," I hesitated, "there'd been that trouble with
Mike, and Dad would've been all alone, and . . . well, I
guess my mind just didn't run to medicine, Bob. It takes
an awful lot of study, you know."

"There's other things you could do, and you lack a lot
of bein' broke, son. You could get you a little fortune for
this property."

"Yeah, but . . ." I broke off. "Well, to tell the truth,
Bob, I have kind of thought about pulling up stakes,
but—"

"Amy don't want to?"

"I haven't asked her. The subject never came up. But I
don't reckon she would."

"Well," he said slowly, "that's sure too bad. I don't
suppose you'd . . . No, you wouldn't do that. I don't expect no man in his right mind would give up Amy."

I nodded a little, like I was acknowledging a compli-
ment; agreeing that I couldn't give her up. And even with
the way I felt about her, the nod came easy. On the surface, Amy had everything plus. She was smart and she
came from a good family—which was a mighty important
consideration with our people. But that was only the beginning. When Amy went down the street with that round

little behind twitching, with her chin tucked in and her breasts stuck out, every man under eighty kind of drooled. They'd get sort of red in the face and forget to breathe, and you could hear whispers, *"Man, if I could just have some of that."*

Hating her didn't keep me from being proud of her.

"You trying to get rid of me, Bob?" I said.

"Kind of looks as though, don't it?" he grinned. "Guess I did too much thinkin' while I was laying around the house. Wondering about things that ain't none of my business. I got to thinkin' about how riled I get sometimes, having to give in to things I don't like, and hell, I ain't really fit to do much but what I am doin'; and I thought how much harder it must be on a man like you." He chuckled, wryly. "Fact is, I reckon, you started me thinking that way, Lou. You kind of brought it on yourself."

I looked blank, and then I grinned. "I don't mean anything by it. It's just a way of joking."

"Sure," he said, easily. "We all got our little pe-cul-ye-arities. I just thought maybe you was gettin' kind of saddle-galled, and—"

"Bob," I said, "what did Conway say to you there in Fort Worth?"

"Oh, hell"—he stood up, slapping his hat against his pants—"can't even recollect what it was now. Well, I guess I better be—"

"He said something. He said or did something that you didn't like a little bit."

"You reckon he did, huh?" His eyebrows went up. Then

they came down and he chuckled, and put on his hat. "Forget it, Lou. It wasn't nothing important, and it don't matter no more, anyways."

He left; and, like I said, I was kind of worried for a while. But after I'd had time to think, it looked to me like I'd fretted about nothing. It looked like things were working out pretty good.

I was willing to leave Central City; I'd been thinking about leaving. But I thought too much of Amy to go against her wishes. I sure wouldn't do anything that Amy didn't like.

If something should happen to her, though—and something *was* going to happen—why, of course, I wouldn't want to hang around the old familiar scenes any more. It would be more than a softhearted guy like me could stand, and there wouldn't be any reason to. So I'd leave, and it'd all seem perfectly natural. No one would think anything of it.

Amy came to see me every day—in the morning for a few minutes on her way to school, and again at night. She always brought some cake or pie or something, stuff I reckon their dog wouldn't eat (and that hound wasn't high-toned—he'd snatch horseturds on the fly), and she hardly nagged about anything, that I remember. She didn't give me any trouble at all. She was all sort of blushy and shy and shamed like. And she had to take it kind of easy when she sat down.

Two or three nights she drew the bathtub full of warm water and sat in it and soaked; and I'd sit and watch her and think how much she looked like *her*. And afterwards she'd lie in my arms—just lie there because that was about all either of us was up to. And I could almost fool myself into thinking it was *her*.

But it wasn't *her*, and, for that matter, it wouldn't have made any difference if it had been. I'd just been right back where I started. I'd have had to do it all over again.

I'd have had to kill her the second time. . . .

I was glad Amy didn't bring up the subject of marriage; she was afraid of starting a quarrel, I guess. I'd already been right in the middle of three deaths, and a fourth coming right on top of 'em might look kind of funny. It was too soon for it. Anyway, I hadn't figured out a good safe way of killing her.

You see why I had to kill her, I reckon. Or do you? It was like this:

There wasn't any evidence against me. And even if there was some, quite a bit, I'd be a mighty hard man to stick. I just wasn't that kind of guy, you see. No one would believe I was. Why, hell, they'd been seeing Lou Ford around for years and no one could tell them that good ol' Lou would—

But Lou could do it; Lou could convict himself. All he had to do was skip out on a girl who knew just about everything about him there was to know—who, even without that one wild night, could probably have pieced some plenty-ugly stuff together—and that would be the end of Lou. Everything would fall into place, right back to the time when Mike and I were kids.

As things stood now, she wouldn't let herself think things through. She wouldn't even let herself start to think. She'd cut up some pretty cute skylarks herself, and that had put a check on her thinking. And I was going to be her husband, so everything was all right. Everything had to be all right. . . . But if I ran out on her—well, I knew Amy. That mental block she'd set up would disappear. She'd have the answer that quick—and she wouldn't keep it to herself. Because if she couldn't have me, no one else would.

Yeah, I guess I mentioned that. She and Joyce seemed pretty much alike.

Well, anyway . . .

Anyway, it had to be done, as soon as it safely could be done. And knowing that, that there was just no other way out, kind of made things easier. I stopped worrying, thinking about it, I should say. I tried to be extra pleasant to her. She was getting on my nerves, hanging around so much. But she wouldn't be hanging around long, so I thought I ought to be as nice as I could.

I'd taken sick on a Wednesday. By the next Wednesday I was up, so I took Amy to prayer meeting. Being a school teacher, she kind of had to put in an appearance at those things, now and then, and I sort of enjoy 'em. I pick up lots of good lines at prayer meetings. I asked Amy, I whispered to her, how she'd like to have a little manna on her honey. And she turned red, and kicked me on the ankle. I whispered to her again, asked her if I could Mose-y into her Burning Bush. I told her I was going to take her to my bosom and cleave unto her, and anoint her with precious oils.

She got redder and redder and her eyes watered, but somehow it made her look cute. And it seemed like I'd never seen her with her chin stuck out and her eyes narrowed. Then, she doubled over, burying her face in her songbook; and she shivered and shook and choked, and the minister stood on tiptoe, frowning, trying to figure out where the racket was coming from.

It was one of the best prayer meetings I ever went to.

I stopped and bought some ice cream on the way home, and she was giggling and breaking into snickers all the way. While I made coffee, she dished up the cream; and I took part of a spoonful and chased her around and around the kitchen with it. I finally caught her and put it in her mouth, instead of down her neck like I'd threatened. A little speck of it got on her nose and I kissed it away.

Suddenly, she threw her arms around my neck and began to cry.

"Honey," I said, "don't do that, honey. I was just playing. I was just trying to give you a good time."

"Y-you—big—"

"I know," I said, "but don't say it. Let's don't have any more trouble between us."

"D-don't"—her arms tightened around me, and she looked up through the tears, smiling—"don't you understand? I'm j-just so happy, Lou. So h-happy I c-can't s-s-stand it!" And she burst into tears again.

We left the ice cream and coffee unfinished. I picked her up and carried her into Dad's office, and sat down in Dad's big old chair. We sat there in the dark, her on my lap—sat there until she had to go home. And it was all we wanted; it seemed to be enough. It was enough.

It was a good evening, even if we did have one small spat.

She asked me if I'd seen Chester Conway, and I said I hadn't. She said she thought it was darned funny that he didn't so much as come by and say hello, after what I'd done, and that if she were me she'd tell him so.

"I didn't do anything," I said. "Let's not talk about it."

"Well, I don't care, darling! He thought you'd done quite a bit at the time—couldn't wait to call you up long distance! Now, he's been back in town for almost a week, and he's too busy to—I don't care for my own sake, Lou. It certainly means nothing to me. But—"

"That makes two of us, then."

"You're too easy-going, that's the trouble with you. You let people run over you. You're always—"

"I know," I said. "I think I know it all, Amy. I've got it memorized. The whole trouble is that I won't listen to you—and it seems to me like that's about all I ever get done. I've been listening to you almost since you learned how to talk, and I reckon I can do it a while longer. If it'll make you happy. But I don't think it'll change me much."

She sat up very stiff and straight. Then, she settled back again, still holding herself kind of rigid. She was silent for about the time it takes to count to ten.

"Well, just the same, I—I—"

"Yeah?" I said.

"Oh, be quiet," she said. "Keep still. Don't say anything." And she laughed. And it was a good evening after all.

But it *was* kind of funny about Conway.

15

How long should I wait? That was the question. How long could I wait? How long was it safe?

Amy wasn't crowding me any. She was still pretty shy and skittish, trying to keep that barbed-wire tongue of hers in her mouth—though she wasn't always successful. I figured I could stall her off on marriage indefinitely, but Amy . . . well, it wasn't just Amy. There wasn't anything I could put my finger on, but I had the feeling that things were closing in on me. And I couldn't talk myself out of it.

Every day that passed, the feeling grew stronger.

Conway hadn't come to see me or spoken to me, but that didn't necessarily mean anything. It *didn't* mean anything that I could see. He was busy. He'd never given a whoop in hell for anyone but himself and Elmer. He was the kind of a guy that would drop you when he got a favor, then pick you up again when he needed another one.

He'd gone back to Fort Worth, and he hadn't returned. But that was all right, too. Conway Construction had big offices in Fort Worth. He'd always spent a lot of time there.

Bob Maples? Well, I couldn't see that he was much different than ever. I'd study him as the days drifted by, and I couldn't see anything to fret about. He looked pretty old and sick, but he *was* old and he had been sick. He didn't have too much to say to me, but what he did have was polite and friendly—he seemed hell-bent on being polite and friendly. And he'd never been what you'd call real talky. He'd always had spells when you could hardly get a word out of him.

Howard Hendricks? Well . . . Well, something was sure enough eating on Howard.

I'd run into Howard the first day I was up after my sick spell; he'd been coming up the steps of the courthouse, just as I was heading down them to lunch. He nodded, not quite looking at me, and mumbled out a, "H'are you, Lou?" I stopped and said I was feeling a lot better—still felt pretty weak, but couldn't really complain any.

"You know how it is, Howard," I said. "It isn't the flu so much as the aftereffects."

"So I've heard," he said.

"It's kind of like I always say about auty-mobiles. It's not the original cost so much as the upkeep. But I reckon—"

"Got to run," he mumbled. "See you."

But I wasn't letting him off that easy. I was really in the clear, now, and I could afford to open up a little on him. "As I was sayin'," I said, "I reckon I can't tell you much about sickness, can I, Howard? Not with that shrapnel you got in you. I got an idea about that shrapnel, How-ard—what you could do with it. You could get you some X-rays taken and print 'em on the back of your campaign cards. Then on the other side you could have a flag with your name spelled out in thermometers, and maybe a up-side down—what do you call them hospital pisspots? Oh, yeah—urinal for an exclamation mark. Where'd you say that shrapnel was anyway, Howard? Seems like I just can't keep track of it, no matter how hard I try. One time it's in—"

"My ass"—he was looking at me now, all right—"it's in my ass."

I'd been holding him by the lapel to keep him from running off. He took my hand by the wrist, still staring at me, and he pulled it away and let it drop. Then, he turned and went up the steps, his shoulders sagging a little but his feet moving firm and steady. And we hadn't passed a word between us since then. He kept out of my way when he saw me coming, and I did him the same kind of favor.

So there was something wrong there; but what else could I expect? What was there to worry about? I'd given him the works, and it had probably dawned on him that I'd needled him plenty in the past. And that wasn't the only reason he had to act stiff and cold. Elections were coming up in the fall, and he'd be running as usual. Break-ing the Conway case would be a big help to him, and he'd want to talk it up. But he'd feel awkward about doing it. He'd have to cut me out of the credit, and he figured I'd be sore. So he was jumping the gun on me.

There was nothing really out of the way, then. Nothing with him or Sheriff Bob or Chester Conway. There wasn't a thing . . . but the feeling kept growing. It got stronger and stronger.

I'd been keeping away from the Greek's. I'd even stayed off the street where his restaurant was. But one day I went there. Something just seemed to pull the wheels of my car in that direction, and I found myself stopping in front of it.

The windows were all soaped over. The doors were closed. But it seemed like I could hear people inside; I heard some banging and clattering.

I got out of my car and stood by the side of it a minute or two. Then, I stepped up on the curb and crossed the walk.

There was a place on one of the double doors where the soap had been scraped away. I sheltered my eyes with my hand and peered through it; rather I started to peer through it. For the door opened suddenly, and the Greek stepped out.

"I am sorry, Officer Ford," he said. "I cannot serve you. We are not open for business."

I stammered that I didn't want anything. "Just thought I'd drop by to—to—"

"Yes?"

I wanted to see you," I said. "I wanted to see you the night it happened, and it hasn't been off my mind since. But I couldn't bring myself to do it. I couldn't face you. I knew how you'd feel, how you'd be bound to feel, and there wasn't anything I could say. Nothing. Nothing I could say or do. Because if there'd been anything . . . well, it wouldn't have happened in the first place."

It was the truth, and God—God!—what a wonderful thing truth is. He looked at me in a way I didn't like to name; and then he looked kind of baffled; and then he suddenly caught his lip under his teeth and stared down at the sidewalk.

He was a swarthy middle-aged guy in a high-crowned black hat, and a shirt with black sateen protectors pulled over the sleeves; and he stared down at the sidewalk and looked back up again.

"I am glad you did come by, Lou," he said, quietly. "It is fitting. I have felt, at times, that he regarded you as his one true friend."

"I aimed to be his friend," I said. "There weren't many things I wanted much more. Somehow, I slipped up; I couldn't help him right when he needed help worst. But I want you to know one thing, Max. I—I didn't hurt—"

He laid a hand on my arm. "You need not tell me that, Lou. I do not know why—what—but—"

"He felt lost," I said. "Like he was all alone in the world. Like he was out of step, and he could never get back in again."

"Yes," he said. "But . . . yes. There was always trouble, and he seemed always at fault."

I nodded, and he nodded. He shook his head, and I shook mine. We stood there, shaking our heads and nodding, neither of us really saying anything; and I wished I could leave. But I didn't quite know how to go about it. Finally, I said I was sorry he was closing the restaurant.

"If there's anything I can do. . . ."

"I am not closing it," he said. "Why should I close it?"

"Well, I just thought that—"

"I am remodeling it. I am putting in leather booths and an inlaid floor and air-conditioning. Johnnie would have liked those things. Many times he suggested them, and I suggested he was hardly fitted to give me advice. But now we will have them. It will be as he wanted. It is—all that can be done."

I shook my head again. I shook it and nodded.

"I want to ask you a question, Lou. I want you to answer it, and I want the absolute truth."

"The truth?" I hesitated. "Why wouldn't I tell you the truth, Max?"

"Because you might feel that you couldn't. That it would be disloyal to your position and associates. Who else visited Johnnie's cell after you left?"

"Well, there was Howard—the county attorney—"

"I know of that; he made the discovery. And a deputy sheriff and the jailer were with him. Who else?"

My heart gave a little jump. Maybe . . . But, no, it was no good. I couldn't do that. I couldn't bring myself to try it.

"I don't have any idea, Max," I said. "I wasn't there. But I can tell you you're on the wrong track. I've known all those boys for years. They wouldn't do a thing like that any more than I would."

It was the truth again, and he had to see it. I was looking straight into his eyes.

"Well . . ." he sighed. "Well, we will talk again, Lou."

And I said, "You bet we will, Max," and I got away from him.

I drove out on Derrick Road, five-six miles out. I pulled the car off on the shoulder, up at the crest of a little hill; and I sat there looking down through the blackjacks but I didn't see a thing. I didn't see the blackjacks.

About five minutes after I'd stopped, well, maybe no more than three minutes, a car drew up behind mine. Joe Rothman got out of it, and plodded along the shoulder and looked in at me.

"Nice view here," he said. "Mind if I join you? Thanks, I knew you wouldn't." He said it like that, all run together, without waiting for me to reply. He opened the door and slid into the seat beside me.

"Come out this way often, Lou?"

"Whenever I feel like it," I said.

"Well, it's a nice view all right. Almost unique. I don't suppose you'll find more than forty or fifty thousand billboards like that one in the United States."

I grinned in spite of myself. The billboard had been put up by the Chamber of Commerce; and the words on it were:

> You are Now Nearing
> C E N T R A L   C I T Y , T E X .
> *"Where the hand clasp's a little stronger."*
> Pop. (1932) 4,800   Pop. (1952) 48,000
> WATCH US GROW!!

"Yeah," I said, "that's quite a sign, all right."

"You were looking at it, then? I thought that must be

the attraction. After all, what else is there to see aside from those blackjacks and a little white cottage? The murder cottage, I believe they call it."

"What do you want?" I said.

"How many times were you there, Lou? How many times did you lay her?"

"I was there quite a few times," I said. "I had reason to be. And I'm not so hard up for it that I have to lay whores."

"No?" He squinted at me thoughtfully. "No, I don't suppose you would be. Personally, I've always operated on the theory that even in the presence of abundance, it's well to keep an eye out for the future. You never can tell, Lou. You may wake up some morning and find they've passed a law against it. It'll be un-American."

"Maybe they'll put a rider on that law," I said.

"Prohibiting bullshit? I see you don't have a legal type of mind, Lou, or you wouldn't say that. There's a basic contradiction in it. Tail we can do without, as our penal institutions so righteously prove; tail of the orthodox type, that is. But what could you substitute for bullshit? Where would we be without it?"

"Well," I said, "I wouldn't be listening to you."

"But you're going to listen to me, Lou. You're going to sit right here and listen, and answer up promptly when the occasion demands. Get me? Get me, Lou?"

"I get you," I said. "I got you right from the beginning."

"I was afraid you hadn't. I wanted you to understand that I can stack it up over your head, and you'll sit there and like it."

He shook tobacco into a paper, twirled it, and ran it across his tongue. He stuck it in the corner of his mouth, and seemed to forget about it.

"You were talking with Max Pappas," he said. "From what I could judge it was a reasonably friendly conversation."

"It was," I said.

"He was resigned to the fact of Johnnie's suicide? He had accepted it as suicide?"

"I can't say that he was resigned to it," I said. "He was wondering whether someone—if someone was in the cell after I left, and . . ."

"And, Lou? And?"

"I told him, no, that it couldn't have been that way. None of the boys would be up to doing such a thing."

"Which settles that," Rothman nodded. "Or does it?"

"What are you driving at?" I snapped. "What—"

"Shut up!" His voice toughened, then went smooth again. "Did you notice the remodeling he's doing? Do you know how much all that will cost? Right around twelve thousand dollars. Where do you suppose he got that kind of money?"

"How the hell do I—"

"Lou."

"Well, maybe he had it saved."

"Max Pappas?"

"Or maybe he borrowed it."

"Without collateral?"

"Well . . . I don't know," I said.

"Let me make a suggestion. Someone gave it to him. A

wealthy acquaintance, we'll say. Some man who felt he owed it to him."

I shrugged, and pushed my hat back; because my forehead was sweating. But I was feeling cold inside, so cold inside.

"Conway Construction is handling the job, Lou. Doesn't it strike you as rather odd that he'd do a job for a man whose son killed his son."

"There aren't many jobs that he don't handle," I said. "Anyway, it's the company, not him; he's not in there swinging a hammer himself. More'n likely he doesn't even know about it."

"Well . . ." Rothman hesitated. Then he went on, kind of dogged. "It's a turnkey job. Conway's jobbing all the materials, dealing with the supply houses, paying off the men. No one's seen a nickel coming from Pappas."

"So what?" I said. "Conway takes all the turnkey stuff he can get. He cuts a half a dozen profits instead of one."

"And you think Pappas would hold still for it? You don't see him as the kind of guy who'd insist on bargaining for every item, who'd haggle over everything right down to the last nail? I see him that way, Lou. It's the only way I can see him."

I nodded. "So do I. But he's not in a real good position to have his own way right now. He gets his job like Conway Construction wants to give it to him, or he just don't get it."

"Yeah . . ." He shifted his cigarette from one side of his mouth to the other. He pushed it across with his tongue, his eyes narrowed on my face. "But the money, Lou. That still doesn't explain about the money."

"He lived close," I said. "He could have had it, a big enough part, anyway, so's they'd wait on the rest. It didn't need to be in a bank. He could have had it salted away around his house."

"Yeah," said Rothman, slowly. "Yeah, I suppose so . . ."

He turned back around in the seat, so that he was looking through the windshield instead of me—instead of *at* me. He flicked his cigarette away, fumbled for his tobacco and papers, and began rolling another one.

"Did you get out to the cemetery, Lou? Out to Johnnie's grave?"

"No," I said, "and I've sure got to do that, too. I'm ashamed I haven't done it before."

"Well—dammit, you mean that, don't you? You mean every word of it!"

"Who are you to ask that?" I snapped. "What did you ever do for him? I don't want any credit for it, but I'm the only man in Central City that ever tried to help that kid. I liked him. I understood him. I—"

"I know, I know," he shook his head, dully. "I was just going to say that Johnnie's buried in Sacred Ground. . . . You know what that means, Lou?"

"I reckon. The church didn't call it suicide."

"And the answer, Lou? You do have an answer?"

"He was so awful young," I said, "and he hadn't ever had much but trouble. Maybe the church figured he'd been faulted enough, and tried to give him a break. Maybe they figured that it was sort of an accident; that he'd just been fooling around and went too far."

"Maybe," said Rothman. "Maybe, maybe, maybe. One more thing, Lou. The big thing . . . On the Sunday night that Elmer and the late occupant of yon cottage got it, one of my carpenters went to the last show at the Palace. He parked his car around in back at—now get this, Lou— at nine-thirty. When he came out, all four of his tires were gone . . ."

16

I waited and everything got pretty quiet. "Well," I said, finally, "that's sure too bad. All four tires, huh?"

"Too bad? You mean it's funny, don't you, Lou? Plumb funny?"

"Well, it is, kind of," I said. "It's funny I didn't hear anything about it at the office."

"It'd been still funnier if you had, Lou. Because he didn't report the theft. I'd hardly call it the greatest mystery of all time, but, for some reason, you fellas down at the office don't take much interest in us fellas down at the labor temple—unless you find us on a picket line."

"I can't hardly help—"

"Never mind, Lou; it's really not pertinent. The man didn't report the theft, but he did mention it to some of the boys when the carpenters and joiners held their regular Tuesday night meeting. And one of them, as it turned out, had bought two of the tires from Johnnie Pappas. They. . . . Do you have a chill, Lou? Are you catching cold?"

I bit down on my cigar. I didn't say anything.

"These lads equipped themselves with a couple of piss-elm clubs, or reasonable facsimiles thereof, and went calling on Johnnie. He wasn't at home and he wasn't at Slim Murphy's filling station. In fact, he wasn't anywhere about that time; he was swinging by his belt from the window-bars of the courthouse cooler. But his hotrod was at the station, and the remaining two stolen tires were on it. They stripped them off—Murphy, of course, isn't confiding in the police either—and that ended the matter. But there's been talk about it, Lou. There's been talk even though—*apparently*—no one has attached any great significance to the event."

I cleared my throat. "I—why should they, Joe?" I said. "I guess I don't get you."

"For the birds, Lou, remember? The starving sparrows. . . . Those tires were stolen after nine-thirty on the night of Elmer's and his lady friend's demise. Assuming that Johnnie didn't go to work on them the moment the owner parked—or even assuming that he did—we are driven to the inevitable conclusion that he was engaged in relatively innocent pursuits until well after ten o'clock. He could not, in other words, have had any part in the horrible happenings behind yonder blackjacks."

"I don't see why not," I said.

"You don't?" His eyes widened. "Well, of course, poor old Descartes, Aristotle, Diogenes, Euclid et al. are dead, but I think you'll find quite a few people around who'll defend their theories. I'm very much afraid, Lou, that they won't go along with your proposition that a body can be in two places at the same time."

"Johnnie ran with a pretty wild crowd," I said. "I figure that one of his buddies stole those tires and gave 'em to him to peddle."

"I see. I see . . . Lou."

"Why not?" I said. "He was in a good position to get rid of them there at the station. Slim Murphy wouldn't have interfered. . . . Why, hell, it's bound to have been that way, Joe. If he'd have had an alibi for the time of the murders, he'd have told me so, wouldn't he? He wouldn't have hanged himself."

"He liked you, Lou. He trusted you."

"For damned good reasons. He knew I was his friend."

Rothman swallowed, and a sort of laughing sound came out of his throat, the kind of sound you make when you don't quite know whether to laugh or cry or get sore.

"Fine, Lou. Perfect. Every brick is laid straight, and the bricklayer is an honest upstanding mechanic. But still I can't help wondering about his handiwork and him. I can't help wondering why he feels the need to defend his structure of perhapses and maybes, his shelter wall of logical alternatives. I can't see why he didn't tell a certain labor skate to get the hell on about his business."

So . . . So there it was. I was. But where was he? He nodded as though I'd asked him the question. Nodded, and drew a little bit back in the seat.

"Humpty-Dumpty Ford," he said, "sitting right on top of the labor temple. And how or why he got there doesn't make much difference. You're going to have to move, Lou. Fast. Before someone . . . before you upset yourself."

"I was kind of figuring on leaving town," I said. "I haven't done anything, but—"

"Certainly you haven't. Otherwise, as a staunch Red Fascist Republican, I wouldn't feel free to yank you from the clutches of your detractors and persecutors—your would-be persecutors, I should say."

"You think that—you think maybe—"

He shrugged, "I think so, Lou. I think you just might have a little trouble in leaving. I think it so strongly that I'm getting in touch with a friend of mine, one of the best criminal lawyers in the country. You've probably heard of him—Billy Boy Walker? I did Billy Boy a favor one time, back East, and he has a long memory for favors, regardless of his other faults."

I'd heard of Billy Boy Walker. I reckon almost everyone has. He'd been governor of Alabama or Georgia or one of those states down south. He'd been a United States senator. He'd been a candidate for president on a Divide-the-Dough ticket. He'd started getting shot at quite a bit about that time, so he'd dropped out of politics and stuck to his criminal law practice. And he was plenty good. All the high mucky-mucks cussed and made fun of him for the way he'd cut up in politics. But I noticed that when they or their kin got into trouble, they headed straight for Billy Boy Walker.

It sort of worried me that Rothman thought I needed that kind of help.

It worried me, and it made me wonder all over again why Rothman and his unions would go to all the trouble of getting me a lawyer. Just what did Rothman stand to lose if the Law started asking me questions? Then I realized that if my first conversation with Rothman should ever come out, any jury in the land would figure he'd sicked me on the late Elmer Conway. In other words, Rothman was saving two necks—his and mine—with one lawyer.

"Perhaps you won't need him," he went on. "But it's best to have him alerted. He's not a man who can make himself available on a moment's notice. How soon can you leave town?"

I hesitated. Amy. How was I going to do it? "I'll—I can't do it right away," I said. "I'll have to kind of drop a hint or two around that I've been thinking about leaving, then work up to it gradually. You know, it would look pretty funny—"

"Yeah," he frowned, "but if they know you're getting ready to jump they're apt to close in all the faster. . . . Still, I can see your point."

"What can they do?" I said. "If they could close in, they'd be doing it already. Not that I've done—"

"Don't bother. Don't say it again. Just move—start moving as quickly as you can. It shouldn't take you more than a couple of weeks at the outside."

Two weeks. Two weeks more for Amy.

"All right, Joe," I said. "And thanks for—for—"

"For what?" He opened the door. "For you, I haven't done a thing."

"I'm not sure I can make it in two weeks. It may take a little—"

"It hadn't better," he said, "take much longer."

He got out and went back to his own car. I waited until he'd turned around and headed back toward Central City; and then I turned around and started back. I drove slowly, thinking about Amy.

Years ago there was a jeweler here in Central City who had a hell of a good business, and a beautiful wife and two fine kids. And one day, on a business trip over to one of the teachers' college towns he met up with a girl, a real honey, and before long he was sleeping with her. She knew he was married, and she was willing to leave it that way. So everything was perfect. He had her and he had his family and a swell business. But one morning they found him and the girl dead in a motel—he'd shot her and killed himself. And when one of our deputies went to tell his wife about it, he found her and the kids dead, too. This fellow had shot 'em all.

He'd had everything, and somehow nothing was better.

That sounds pretty mixed up, and probably it doesn't have a lot to do with me. I thought it did at first, but now that I look at it—well, I don't know. I just don't know.

I knew I had to kill Amy; I could put the reason into words. But every time I thought about it, I had to stop and think *why* again. I'd be doing something, reading a book or something, or maybe I'd be with her. And all of a sudden it would come over me that I was going to kill her, and the idea seemed so crazy that I'd almost laugh out loud. Then, I'd start thinking and I'd see it, see that it had to be done, and . . .

It was like being asleep when you were awake and awake when you were asleep. I'd pinch myself, figuratively speaking—I had to keep pinching myself. Then I'd wake up kind of in reverse; I'd go back into the nightmare I had to live in. And everything would be clear and reasonable.

But I still didn't know how to go about doing it. I couldn't figure out a way that would leave me in the clear or even reasonably in the clear. And I sure had to be on this one. I was Humpty-Dumpty, like Rothman had said, and I couldn't jiggle around very much.

I couldn't think of a way because it was a real toughie, and I had to keep remembering the *why* of it. But finally it came to me.

I found a way, because I had to. I couldn't stall any longer.

It happened three days after my talk with Rothman. It was a payday Saturday, and I should have been working, but somehow I hadn't been able to bring myself to do it. I'd stayed in the house all day with the shades drawn, pacing back and forth, wandering from room to room. And when night came I was still there. I was sitting in Dad's office, with nothing on but the little desk light; and I heard these footsteps moving lightly across the porch, and the sound of the screen door opening.

It was way too early for Amy; but I wasn't jittered any. I'd had people walk in before like this.

I stepped to the door of the office just as he came into the hall.

"I'm sorry, stranger," I said. "The doctor doesn't practice any more. The sign's just there for sentimental reasons."

"That's okay, bud"—he walked right toward me and I had to move back—"it's just a little burn."

"But I don't—"

"A cigar burn," he said. And he held his hand out, palm up.

And, at last, I recognized him.

He sat down in Dad's big leather chair, grinning at me. He brushed his hand across the arm, knocking off the coffee cup and saucer I'd left there.

"We got some talking to do, bud, and I'm thirsty. You got some whiskey around? An unopened bottle? I ain't no whiskey hog, understand, but some places I like to see a seal on a bottle."

"I've got a phone around," I said, "and the jail's about six blocks away. Now, drag your ass out of here before you find yourself in it."

"Huh-uh," he said. "You want to use that phone, go right ahead, bud."

I started to. I figured he'd be afraid to go through with it, and if he did, well, my word was still better than any bum's. No one had anything on me, and I was still Lou Ford. And he wouldn't get his mouth open before someone smacked a sap in it.

"Go 'head, bud, but it'll cost you. It'll sure cost you. And it won't be just the price of a burned hand."

I held onto the phone, but I didn't lift the receiver. "Go on," I said, "let's have it."

"I got interested in you, bud. I spent a year stretch on the Houston pea farm, and I seen a couple guys like you there; and I figured it might pay to watch you a little. So

I followed you that night. I heard some of the talk you had with that labor fellow. . . ."

"And I reckon it meant a hell of a lot to you, didn't it?" I said.

"No, sir," he wagged his head, "hardly meant a thing to me. Fact is, it didn't mean much to me a couple nights later when you came up to that old farm house where I was shacked up, and then cut cross-prairie to that little white house. That didn't mean much neither, *then*. . . . You say you had some whiskey, bud? An unopened bottle?"

I went into the laboratory, and got a pint of old prescription liquor from the stores cabinet. I brought it back with a glass; and he opened it and poured the glass half full.

"Have one on the house," he said, and handed it to me.

I drank it; I needed it. I passed the glass back to him, and he dropped it on the floor with the cup and saucer. He took a big swig from the bottle, and smacked his lips.

"No, sir," he went on, "it didn't mean a thing, and I couldn't stick around to figure it out. I hiked out of there, early Monday morning, and hit up the pipeline for a job. They put me with a jackhammer crew way the hell over on the Pecos, so far out I couldn't make town my first payday. Just three of us there by ourselves cut off from the whole danged world. But this payday it was different. We'd finished up on the Pecos, and I got to come in. I caught up on the news, bud, and those things you'd done and said meant plenty."

I nodded. I felt kind of glad. It was out of my hands,

now, and the pieces were falling into place. I knew I had to do it, and how I was going to do it.

He took another swallow of whiskey and dug a cigarette from his shirt pocket. "I'm an understandin' man, bud, and the law ain't helped me none and I ain't helpin' it none. Unless I have to. What you figure it's worth to you to go on living?"

"I—" I shook my head. I had to go slow. I couldn't give in too easily. "I haven't got much money," I said. "Just what I make on my job."

"You got this place. Must be worth a pretty tidy sum, too."

"Yeah, but, hell," I said. "It's all I've got. If I'm not going to have a window left to throw it out of, there's not much percentage in keeping you quiet."

"You might change your mind about that, bud," he said. But he didn't sound too firm about it.

"Anyway," I said, "it's just not practical to sell it. People would wonder what I'd done with the money. I'd have to account for it to the government and pay a big chunk of taxes on it. For that matter—I reckon you're in kind of a hurry—"

"You reckon right, bud."

"Well, it would take quite a while to get rid of a place like this. I'd want to sell it to a doctor, someone who'd pay for my Dad's practice and equipment. It'd be worth at least a third more that way, but the deal couldn't be swung in a hurry."

He studied me, suspiciously, trying to figure out how

much if any I was stringing him. As a matter of fact, I wasn't lying more'n a little bit.

"I don't know," he said slowly. "I don't know much about them things. Maybe—you reckon you could swing a loan on it?"

"Well, I'd sure hate to do that—"

"That ain't what I asked you, bud."

"But, look," I said, making it good, "how would I pay it back out of my job? I just couldn't do it. I probably wouldn't get more than five thousand after they took out interest and brokerage fees. And I'd have to turn right around somewhere and swing another loan to pay off the first one, and—hell, that's no way to do business. Now, if you'll just give me four-five months to find someone who—"

"Huh-uh. How long it take you to swing this loan? A week?"

"Well . . ." I might have to give her a little longer than that. I wanted to give her longer. "I think that'd be a little bit quick. I'd say two weeks; but I'd sure hate—"

"Five thousand," he said, sloshing the whiskey in the bottle. "Five thousand in two weeks. Two weeks from tonight. All right, bud, we'll call that a deal. An' it'll be a deal, understand? I ain't no hog about money or nothin'. I get the five thousand and that's the last we'll see of each other."

I scowled and cussed, but I said, "Well, all right."

He tucked the whiskey into his hip pocket, and stood up. "Okay, bud. I'm going back out to the pipeline tonight. This ain't a very friendly place for easy-livin' men, so I'll stay out there another payday. But don't get no notions about runnin' out on me."

"How the hell could I?" I said. "You think I'm crazy?"

"You ask unpleasant questions, bud, and you may get unpleasant answers. Just be here with that five grand two weeks from tonight and there won't be no trouble."

I gave him a clincher; I still felt I might be giving in too easy. "Maybe you'd better not come here," I said. "Someone might see you and—"

"No one will. I'll watch myself like I did tonight. I ain't no more anxious for trouble than you are."

"Well," I said, "I just thought it might be better if we—"

"Now, bud"—he shook his head—"what happened the last time you was out wanderin' around old empty farm houses? It didn't turn out so good, did it?"

"All right," I said. "Suit yourself about it."

"That's just what I aim to do." He glanced toward the clock. "We got it all straight, then. Five thousand, two weeks from tonight, nine o'clock. That's it, and don't slip up on it."

"Don't worry. You'll get it," I said.

He stood at the front door a moment, sizing up the situation outside. Then he slipped out and off of the porch, and disappeared in the trees on the lawn.

I grinned, feeling a little sorry for him. It was funny the way these people kept asking for it. Just latching onto you, no matter how you tried to brush them off, and almost telling you how they wanted it done. Why'd they all have to come to me to get killed? Why couldn't they kill themselves?

I cleaned up the broken dishes in the office. I went upstairs and lay down and waited for Amy. I didn't have long to wait.

I didn't have long; and in a way she was the same as always, sort of snappy and trying not to be. But I could sense a difference, the stiffness that comes when you want to say or do something and don't know how to begin. Or maybe she could sense it in me; maybe we sensed it in each other.

I guess that's the way it was, because we both came out with it together. We spoke at the same time:

"Lou, why don't we . . ." } we said.
"Amy, why don't we . . ." }

We laughed and said "bread and butter," and then she spoke again.

"You do want to, don't you, darling? Honest and truly?"

"Didn't I just start to ask you?" I said.

"How—when do you—"

"Well, I was thinking a couple of weeks would—"

"Darling!" She kissed me. "That was just what I was going to say!"

There was just a little more. That last piece of the picture needed one more little push.

"What are you thinking about, darling?"

"Well, I was thinking we've always had to do kinda like people expected us to. I mean—Well, what were you thinking about?"

"You tell me first, Lou."

"No, you tell me, Amy."

"Well . . ."

"Well . . ."

"Why don't we elope," we said.

We laughed, and she threw her arms around me, snuggled up against me, sort of shivery but warm; so hard but so soft. And she whispered into my ear and I whispered into hers:

"Bread and butter . . ."

"Bad luck, stay 'way from my darling."

17

He showed up on, well, I guess it was the following Tuesday. The Tuesday after the Saturday the bum had shown up and Amy and I had decided to elope. He was a tall, stoop-shouldered guy with a face that seemed to be all bone and yellowish tightly drawn skin. He said his name was Dr. John Smith and that he was just passing through; he was just looking around in this section, and he'd heard—he'd thought, perhaps—that the house and the practice might be on the market.

It was around nine o'clock in the morning. By rights, I should have been headed for the courthouse. But I wasn't knocking myself out, these days, to get downtown; and Dad had always laid himself out for any doctors that came around.

"I've thought about selling it, off and on," I said, "but that's about as far as it's gone. I've never taken any steps in that direction. But come in, anyway. Doctors are always welcome in this house."

I sat him down in the office and brought out a box of cigars, and got him some coffee. Then, I sat down with him and tried to visit. I can't say that I liked him much. He kept staring at me out of his big yellow eyes like I was really some sort of curiosity, something to look at instead of to talk to. But—well, doctors get funny mannerisms. They live in an I'm-the-King world, where everyone else is wrong but them.

"You're a general practitioner, Doctor Smith?" I said. "I wouldn't want to discourage you, but I'm afraid the general practice field is pretty well the monopoly here of long-established doctors. Now—I haven't thought too much about disposing of this place, but I might consider it—now, I do think there's room for a good man in pediatrics or obstetrics. . . ."

I let it hang there, and he blinked and came out of his trance.

"As a matter of fact, I am interested in those fields, Mr. Ford. I would—uh—hesitate to call myself a specialist, but—uh—"

"I think you might find an opening here, then," I said. "What's been your experience in treating nephritis, doctor? Would you say that inoculation with measles has sufficiently proven itself as a curative agent to warrant the inherent danger?"

"Well, uh—uh—" He crossed his legs. "Yes and no."

I nodded seriously. "You feel that there are two sides to the question?"

"Well—uh—yes."

"I see," I said. "I'd never thought about it quite that way, but I can see that you're right."

"That's your—uh—specialty, Mr. Ford? Children's diseases?"

"I haven't any specialty, doctor," I laughed. "I'm living proof of the adage about the shoemaker's son going barefooted. But I've always been interested in children, and I suppose the little I do know about medicine is confined to pediatrics."

"I see. Well, uh, as a matter of fact, most of my work has been in—uh—geriatrics."

"You should do well here, then," I said. "We have a high percentage of elderly people in the population. Geriatrics, eh?"

"Well, uh, as a matter of fact . . ."

"You know *Max Jacobsohn on Degenerative Diseases?* What do you think of his theorem as to the ratio between decelerated activity and progressive senility? I can understand the basic concept, of course, but my math isn't good enough to allow me to appreciate his formulae. Perhaps you'll explain them to me?"

"Well, I—uh—it's pretty complicated. . . ."

"I see. You feel, perhaps, that Jacobsohn's approach may be a trifle empirical? Well, I was inclined to that belief myself, for a time, but I'm afraid it may have been because my own approach was too subjective. For instance. Is the condition pathological? Is it psychopathological? Is it psycho-pathological-psychosomatic? Yes, yes, yes. It can be one or two or all three—*but* in varying degrees, doctor. Like it or not, we must contemplate an x factor. Now, to strike an equation—and you'll pardon me for oversimplifying—let's say that our cosine is . . ."

I went on smiling and talking, wishing that Max Jacob-sohn was here to see him. From what I'd heard of Dr. Jacobsohn, he'd probably grab this guy by the seat of his pants and boot him out into the street.

"As a matter of fact," he interrupted me, rubbing a big bony hand across his forehead, "I have a very bad head-ache. What do you do for headaches, Mr. Ford."

"I never have them," I said.

"Uh, oh? I thought perhaps that studying so much, sit-ting up late nights when you can't—uh—sleep . . ."

"I never have any trouble sleeping," I said.

"You don't worry a lot? I mean that in a town such as this where there is so much gossip—uh—malicious gossip, you don't feel that people are talking about you? It doesn't—uh—seem unbearable at times?"

"You mean," I said slowly, "do I feel persecuted? Well, as a matter of fact, I do, doctor. But I never worry about it. I can't say that it doesn't bother me, but—"

"Yes? Yes, Mr. Ford?"

"Well, whenever it gets too bad, I just step out and kill a few people. I frig them to death with a barbed-wire cob I have. After that I feel fine."

I'd been trying to place him, and finally it had come to me. It's been several years since I'd seen that big ugly mug in one of the out-of-town papers, and the picture hadn't been so good a resemblance. But I remembered it, now, and some of the story I'd read about him. He'd taken his degree at the University of Edinburgh at a time when we were admitting their graduates to practice. He'd killed half a dozen people before he picked up a jerkwater Ph.D., and edged into psychiatry.

Out on the West Coast, he'd worked himself into some staff job with the police. And then a big murder case had cropped up, and he'd gotten hog-wild raw with the wrong suspects—people who had the money and influence to fight back. He hadn't lost his license, but he'd had to skip out fast. Now, well, I knew what he'd be doing now. What he'd have to be doing. Lunatics can't vote, so why should the legislature vote a lot of money for them?

"As a matter of fact—uh—" It was just beginning to soak in on him. "I think I'd better—"

"Stick around," I said. "I'll show you that corncob. Or maybe you can show me something from your collection—those Japanese sex goods you used to flash around. What'd you do with that rubber phallus you had? The one you squirted into that high school kid's face? Didn't you have time to pack it when you jumped the Coast?"

"I'm a-afraid you have me confused w-with—"

"As a matter of fact," I said, "I *do*. But you don't have me confused. You wouldn't know how to begin. You wouldn't know shit from wild honey, so go back and sign your report that way. Sign it shitbird. And you'd better add a footnote to the effect that the next son-of-a-bitch they send out here is going to get kicked so hard he'll be wearing his asshole for a collar."

He backed out into the hall and toward the front door, the bones in his face wobbling and twitching under the tight yellow skin. I followed him grinning.

He stuck a hand out sideways and lifted his hat from the hall tree. He put it on backwards; and I laughed and took a quick step toward him. He almost fell out the door; and I picked up his briefcase and threw it into the yard.

"Take care of yourself, doc," I said. "Take good care of your keys. If you ever lose them, you won't be able to get out."

"You—you'll be . . ." The bones were jerking and jumping. He'd got down the steps, and his nerve was coming back. "If I ever get you up—"

"Me, doc? But I sleep swell. I don't have headaches. I'm not worried a bit. The only thing that bothers me is that corncob wearing out."

He snatched up the briefcase and went loping down the walk, his neck stuck out like a buzzard's. I slammed the door, and made more coffee.

I cooked a big second breakfast, and ate it all.

You see, it didn't make a bit of difference. I hadn't lost a thing by telling him off. I'd thought they were closing in on me, and now I knew it. And they'd know that I knew it. But nothing was lost by that, and nothing else had changed.

They could still only guess, suspect. They had no more to go on than they'd ever had. They still wouldn't have anything two weeks—well, ten days from now. They'd have more suspicions, they'd *feel* surer than ever. But they wouldn't have any proof.

They could only find the proof in me—in what I was—and I'd never show it to 'em.

I finished the pot of coffee, smoked a cigar and washed

and wiped the dishes. I tossed some bread scraps into the yard for the sparrows, and watered the sweet potato plant in the kitchen window.

Then, I got out the car and headed for town; and I was thinking how good it had been to talk—even if he had turned out to be phony—for a while. To talk, really talk, for even a little while.

18

I killed Amy Stanton on Saturday night on the fifth of April, 1952, at a few minutes before nine o'clock.

It had been a bright, crisp spring day, just warm enough so's you'd know that summer was coming, and the night was just tolerably cool. And she fixed her folks an early dinner, and got them off to a picture show about seven. Then, at eight-thirty, she came over to my place, and . . .

Well, I saw them going by my house—her folks, I mean—and I guess she must have been standing at their gate waving to 'em, because they were looking back and waving. Then, I guess, she went back into the house and started getting ready real fast; taking her hair down and bathing, and fixing her face and getting her bags packed. I guess she must have been busy as all hell, jumping sideways to get ready, because she hadn't been able to do much while her folks were around. I guess she must have been chasing back and forth, turning on the electric iron, shutting off the bathwater, straightening the seams in her stockings, moving her mouth in and out to center the lipstick while she jerked the pins from her hair.

Why, hell, she had dozens of things to do, dozens of

'em, and if she'd just moved a little bit slower, ever so little—but Amy was one of those quick, sure girls. She was ready with time to spare, I guess, and then—I guess—she stood in front of the mirror, frowning and smiling, pouting and tossing her head, tucking her chin in and looking up under her brows; studying herself frontwards and sidewards, turning around and looking over her shoulder and brushing at her bottom, hitching her girdle up a little and down a little and then gripping it by both sides and sort of wiggling her hips in it. Then . . . then, I guess that must have been about all; she was all ready. So she came over where I was, and I . . .

I was ready, too. I wasn't fully dressed, but I was ready for her.

I was standing in the kitchen waiting for her, and she was out of breath from hurrying so fast, I guess, and her bags were pretty heavy, I guess, and I guess . . .

I guess I'm not ready to tell about it yet. It's too soon, and it's not necessary yet. Because, hell, we had a whole two weeks before then, before Saturday, April 5th, 1952, at a few minutes before nine p.m.

We had two weeks and they were pretty good ones, because for the first time in I don't remember when my mind was really free. The end was coming up, it was rushing toward me, and everything would be over soon. I could think, well, go ahead and say something, do something, and it won't matter now. I can stall you *that* long; and I don't have to watch myself any more.

I was with her every night. I took her everywhere she wanted to go, and did everything she wanted to do. And it wasn't any trouble, because she didn't want to go much or do much. One evening we parked by the high school, and watched the baseball team work out. Another time we went down to the depot to see the Tulsa Flyer go through with the people looking out the dining car windows and the people staring back from the observation car.

That's about all we did, things like that, except maybe to drive down to the confectionery for some ice cream. Most of the time we just stayed at home, at my house. Both of us sitting in Dad's big old chair, or both of us stretched out upstairs, face to face, holding each other.

Just holding each other a lot of nights.

We'd lie there for hours, not speaking for an hour at a time sometimes; but the time didn't drag any. It seemed to rush by. I'd lie there listening to the ticking of the clock, listening to her heart beat with it, and I'd wonder why it had to tick so fast; I'd wonder *why*. And it was hard to wake up and go to sleep, to go back into the nightmare where I could remember.

We had a few quarrels but no bad ones. I just wasn't going to have them; I let her have her own way and she tried to do the same with me.

One night she said she was going to the barbershop with me some time, and see that I got a decent haircut for a change. And I said—before I remembered—whenever she felt like doing that, I'd start wearing it in a braid. So we had a little spat, but nothing bad.

Then, one night she asked me how many cigars I smoked in a day, and I said I didn't keep track of 'em.

She asked me why I didn't smoke cigarettes like "everyone else" did, and I said I didn't reckon that everyone else did smoke 'em. I said there was two members of my family that never smoked 'em, Dad and me. She said, well, of course, if you thought more of him than you do of me, there's nothing more to be said. And I said, Jesus Christ, how do you figure—what's that got to do with it?

But it was just a little spat. Nothing bad at all. I reckon she forgot about it right away like she did the first one.

I think she must have had a mighty good time those two weeks. Better'n any she'd ever had before.

So the two weeks passed, and the night of April fifth came; and she hustled her folks off to a show, and scampered around getting ready, and she got ready. And at eight-thirty she came over to my place and I was waiting for her. And I . . .

But I guess I'm getting ahead of myself again. There's some other things to tell first.

I went to work every working day of those two weeks; and believe me it wasn't easy. I didn't want to face anyone—I wanted to stay there in the house with the shades drawn, and not see anyone at all, and I knew I couldn't do that. I went to work, I forced myself to, just like always.

They suspected me; and I'd let 'em know that I knew. But there wasn't a thing on my conscience; I wasn't afraid of a thing. And I proved that there wasn't by going down. Because how could a man who'd done what they thought I had, go right on about his business and look people in the eye?

I was sore, sure. My feelings were hurt. But I wasn't afraid and I proved it.

Most of the time, at first, anyway, I wasn't given much to do. And believe me that was hard, standing around with my face hanging out and pretending like I didn't notice or give a damn. And when I did get a little job, serving a warrant or something like that, there was always a reason for another deputy to go along with me. He'd be embarrassed and puzzled, because, of course, they were keeping the secret at the top, between Hendricks and Conway and Bob Maples. He'd wonder what was up but he couldn't ask, because, in our own way, we're the politest people in the world; we'll joke around and talk about everything except what's on our minds. But he'd wonder and he'd be embarrassed, and he'd try to brag me up—maybe talk me up about the Johnnie Pappas deal to make me feel better.

I was coming back from lunch one day when the hall floors had just been oiled. And they didn't make much noise when you stepped on them, and when you kind of had to pick your way along they didn't make any at all. Deputy Jeff Plummer and Sheriff Bob were talking, and they didn't hear me coming. So I stopped just short of the door and listened. I listened and I saw them: I knew them so well I could see 'em without looking.

Bob was at his desk, pretending to thumb through some papers; and his glasses were down on the end of his nose, and he was looking up over them now and then. And he didn't like what he had to say, but you'd never know it the way his eyes came up over those glasses and the way he talked. Jeff Plummer was hunkered down in one of the windows, studying his fingernails, maybe, his jaws moving on a stick of gum. And he didn't like telling Bob off—and he didn't sound like he was; just easy-going and casual—but he was sure as hell doing it.

"No, sir, Bob," he drawled. "Been kind of studyin' things over, and I reckon I ain't going to do no spying no more. Ain't going to do it a-tall."

"You got your mind made up, huh? You're plumb set?"

"Well, now, it sure looks that way, don't it? Yes, sir, I reckon that's prob'ly the way it is. Can't rightly see it no other way."

"You see how it's possible to do a job if'n you don't follow orders? You reckon you can do that?"

"Now"—Jeff was looking—*looking*—real pleased, like he'd drawn aces to three kings—"now, I'm sure proud you mentioned that, Bob. I plain admire a man that comes square to a point."

There was a second's silence, then a *clink* as Jeff's badge hit the desk. He slid out of the window and sauntered toward the door, smiling but not with his eyes. And Bob cussed and jumped up.

"You ornery coyote! You tryin' to knock my eyes out with that thing? I ever catch you throwin' it around again, I'll whup you down to a nubbin."

Jeff scuffed his boots; he cleared his throat. He said it was a plumb purty day out, and a man'd have to be plain out of his mind to claim different.

"I reckon a man hadn't ought to ask you a question about all the hocus-pocus around here, now had he, Bob? It wouldn't be what you'd call proper?"

"Well, now, I don't know as I'd put it that way. Don't reckon I'd even prod him about why he was askin'. I'd just figure he was a man, and a man just does what he has to."

I slipped into the men's john and stayed there a while. And when I went into the office, Jeff Plummer was gone and Bob gave me a warrant to serve. By myself. He didn't exactly meet my eye, but he seemed pretty happy. He had his neck out a mile—he had everything to lose and nothing to gain—and he was happy.

And I didn't know whether I felt better or not.

Bob didn't have much longer to live, and the job was all he had. Jeff Plummer had a wife and four kids, and he was just about standing in the middle of his wardrobe whenever you saw him. People like that, well, they don't make up their mind about a man in a hurry. But once it's made up they hardly ever change it. They can't. They'd almost rather die than do it.

I went on about my business every day, and things were easier for me in a sense, because people acted easier around me, and twice as hard in another way. Because the folks that trust you, that just won't hear no bad about you nor even think it, those are the ones that are hard to fool. You can't put your heart in the job.

I'd think about my—those people, so many of them, and I'd wonder *why*. I'd have to go through it all again, step by step. And just about the time I'd get it settled, I'd start wondering all over again.

I guess I got kind of sore at myself. And at them. All those people. I'd think, why in the hell did they have to do it—I didn't ask 'em to stick their necks out; I'm not begging for friendship. But they *did* give me their friendship and they *did* stick their necks out. So along toward the last, I was sticking mine out.

I stopped by the Greek's place every day. I looked over the work and had him explain things to me, and I'd offer him a lift when he had to go some place. I'd say it was sure going to be one up-to-date restaurant and that Johnnie would sure like it—that he did like it. Because there hadn't ever been a better boy, and now he could look on, look down, and admire things the same as we could. I said I knew he could, that Johnnie was really happy now.

And the Greek didn't have much to say for a while— he was polite but he didn't say much. Then, pretty soon, he was taking me out in the kitchen for coffee; and he'd walk me clear out to my car when I had to leave. He'd hang around me, nodding and nodding while I talked about Johnnie. And once in a while he'd remember that maybe he ought to be ashamed, and I knew he wanted to apologize but was afraid of hurting my feelings.

Chester Conway had been staying in Fort Worth, but he came back in town one day for a few hours and I made it my business to hear about it. I was driving by his offices real slow, around two in the afternoon, when he came barging out looking for a taxi. And before he knew what was happening, I had him in charge. I hopped out, took his briefcase away from him and hustled him into my car.

It was the last thing he'd've expected of me. He was too set back to talk, and he didn't have time to say anything. And after we were headed for the airport, he didn't get a chance. Because I was doing all the talking.

I said, "I've been hoping to run into you, Mr. Conway. I wanted to thank you for the hospitality you showed me in Fort Worth. It was sure thoughtful of you at a time like that, to think of me and Bob's comfort, and I guess I wasn't so thoughtful myself. I was kind of tired, just thinkin' of my own problems instead of yours, how you must feel, and I reckon I was pretty snappy with you there at the airport. But I didn't really mean anything by it, Mr. Conway, and I've been wanting to apologize. I wouldn't blame you a bit if you were put out with me, because I ain't ever had much sense and I guess I've made a hell of a mess of things.

"Now, I knew Elmer was kind of innocent and trusting and I knew a woman like that just couldn't be much good. I shoulda done like you said and gone there with him—I don't rightly see how I could the way she was acting, but I shoulda done that anyway. And don't think I don't know it now, and if cussing me out will help any or if you want to get my job, and I know you can get it, I won't hold any grudge. No matter what you did it wouldn't be enough, it wouldn't bring Elmer back. An' . . . I never got to know him real well, but in a way kinda I felt like I did. I reckon it must've been because he looked so much like you. I'd see him from a distance some times and I'd think it was you. I guess maybe that's one reason I wanted to see you today. It was kinda like seein' Elmer again. I could sorta feel for a minute that he was still here an' nothing had ever happened. An' . . ."

We'd come to the airport.

He got out without speaking or looking at me, and strode off to the plane. Moving fast, never turning around or looking sideways; almost like he was running away from something.

He started up the ramp, but he wasn't moving so fast now. He was walking slower and slower, and halfway up he almost stopped. Then he went on, plodding, dragging his feet; and he reached the top. And he stood there for a second, blocking the door.

He turned around, gave the briefcase a little jerk, and ducked inside the plane.

He'd waved to me.

I drove back to town, and I guess I gave up about then. It was no use. I'd done everything I could. I'd dropped it in their plates, and rubbed their noses in it. And it was no use. They wouldn't see it.

No one would stop me.

So, on Saturday night, April 5th, 1952, at a few minutes before nine o'clock, I . . .

But I guess there's another thing or two to tell you first, and—but I *will* tell you about it. I want to tell you, and I will, exactly how it happened. I won't leave you to figure things out for yourself.

In lots of books I read, the writer seems to go haywire every time he reaches a high point. He'll start leaving out punctuation and running his words together and babble about stars flashing and sinking into a deep dreamless sea. And you can't figure out whether the hero's laying his girl or a cornerstone. I guess that kind of crap is supposed to be pretty deep stuff—a lot of the book reviewers eat it up, I notice. But the way I see it is, the writer is just too goddam lazy to do his job. And I'm not lazy, whatever else I am. I'll tell you everything.

But I want to get everything in the right order.

I want you to understand how it was.

Late Saturday afternoon, I got Bob Maples alone for a minute and told him I wouldn't be able to work that night. I said that Amy and me had something mighty important to do, and maybe I wouldn't be getting in Monday or Tuesday either; and I gave him a wink.

"Well, now,"—he hesitated, frowning. "Well, now, you don't think maybe that—" Then, he gripped my hand and wrung it. "That's real good news, Lou. Real good. I know you'll be happy together."

"I'll try not to lay off too long," I said. "I reckon things are, well, kind of up in the air and—"

"No, they ain't," he said, sticking his chin out. "Everything's all right, and it's going to stay that way. Now go on and buss Amy for me, and don't you worry about nothing."

It still wasn't real late in the day, so I drove out on Derrick Road and parked a while.

Then I went home, leaving the car parked out in front, and fixed dinner.

I stretched out on the bed for about an hour, letting my food settle. I drew water in the bath tub and got in.

I lay in the tub for almost an hour, soaking and smoking and thinking. Finally, I got out, looked at the clock and began laying out clothes.

I packed my gladstone, and cinched the straps on it. I put on clean underwear and socks and new-pressed pants, and my Sunday go-to-meetin' boots. I left off my shirt and tie.

I sat on the edge of the bed smoking until eight o'clock. Then, I went downstairs to the kitchen.

I turned the light on in the pantry, moving the door back and forth until I had it like I wanted it. Until there was just enough light in the kitchen. I looked around, making sure that all the blinds were drawn, and went into Dad's office.

I took down the concordance to the Bible and removed the four hundred dollars in marked money, Elmer's money. I dumped the drawers of Dad's desk on the floor. I turned off the light, pulled the door almost shut, and went back into the kitchen.

The evening newspaper was spread out on the table. I slid a butcher knife under it, and—And it was that time. I heard her coming.

She came up the back steps and across the porch, and banged and fumbled around for a minute getting the door open. She came in, out of breath kind of and out of temper, and pushed the door shut behind her. And she saw me standing there, not saying anything because I'd forgotten *why* and I was trying to remember. And, finally, I did remember.

So—or did I mention it already?—on Saturday night, the fifth of April, 1952, at a few minutes before nine o'clock I killed Amy Stanton.

Or maybe you could call it suicide.

19

She saw me and it startled her for a second. Then she dropped her two traveling cases on the floor and gave one of 'em a kick, and brushed a wisp of hair from her eyes.

"Well!" she snapped. "I don't suppose it would occur to you to give me a little help! Why didn't you leave the car in the garage, anyway?"

I shook my head. I didn't say anything.

"I'll swear, Lou Ford! Sometimes I think—And you're not even ready yet! You're always talking about how slow I am, and here you stand, on your own wedding night of all things, and you haven't—" She stopped suddenly, her mouth shut tight, her breasts rising and falling. And I heard the kitchen clock tick ten times before she spoke again. "I'm sorry, darling," she said softly. "I didn't mean—"

"Don't say anything more, Amy," I said. "Just don't say anything more."

She smiled and came toward me with her arms held out. "I won't darling. I won't ever say anything like that again. But I do want to tell you how much—"

"Sure," I said. "You want to pour your heart out to me."

And I hit her in the guts as hard as I could.

My fist went back against her spine, and the flesh closed around it to the wrist. I jerked back on it, I had to jerk, and she flopped forward from the waist, like she was hinged.

Her hat fell off, and her head went clear down and touched the floor. And then she toppled over, completely over, like a kid turning a somersault. She lay on her back, eyes bulging, rolling her head from side to side.

She was wearing a white blouse and a light cream-colored suit; a new one, I reckon, because I didn't remember seeing it before. I got my hand in the front of the blouse, and ripped it down to the waist. I jerked the skirt up over her head, and she jerked and shook all over; and there was a funny sound like she was trying to laugh.

And then I saw the puddle spreading out under her.

I sat down and tried to read the paper. I tried to keep my eyes on it. But the light wasn't very good, not good enough to read by, and she kept moving around. It looked like she couldn't lie still.

Once I felt something touch my boot, and I looked down and it was her hand. It was moving back and forth across the toe of my boot. It moved up along the ankle and the leg, and somehow I was afraid to move away. And then her fingers were at the top, clutching down inside; and I almost couldn't move. I stood up and tried to jerk away, and the fingers held on.

I dragged her two-three feet before I could break away.

Her fingers kept on moving, sliding and crawling back and forth, and finally they got ahold of her purse and held on. They dragged it down inside of her skirt, and I couldn't see it or her hands any more.

Well, that was all right. It would look better to have her hanging onto her purse. And I grinned a little, thinking about it. It was so much like her, you know, to latch onto her purse. She'd always been so tight, and . . . and I guess she'd had to be.

There wasn't a better family in town than the Stantons. But both her folks had been ailing for years, and they didn't have much any more aside from their home. She'd had to be tight, like any damned fool ought to have known; because there wasn't any other way of being, and that's all any of us ever are: what we have to be. And I guessed it hadn't been very funny when I'd kidded her dead-pan, and acted surprised when she got mad.

I guess that stuff she'd brought to me when I was sick wasn't really crap. It was as good as she knew how to fix. I guess that dog of theirs didn't have to chase horses un-less'n he wanted the exercise. I—

Why the hell didn't he come? Hell, she hadn't had a real breath now in almost thirty minutes, and it was hard as hell on her. I knew how hard it was and I held my own breath for a while because we'd always done things to-gether, and . . .

He came.

I'd locked the front screen, so that he couldn't just walk in, and I heard him tugging at it.

I gave her two hard kicks in the head and she rose off

the floor, her skirt falling down off of her face, and I knew there wouldn't be any doubt about her. She was dead on the night of—Then I went and opened the door and let him in.

I pushed the roll of marked twenties on him and said, "Stick this in your pocket. I've got the rest back in the kitchen," and I started back there.

I knew he would put the money in his pocket, and you do too if you can remember back when you were a kid. You'd walk up to a guy and say, "Here, hold this," and probably he'd pulled the same gag himself; he'd know you were handing him a horse turd or a prickly pear or a dead mouse. But if you pulled it fast enough, he'd do just what you told him.

I pulled it fast, and headed right back toward the kitchen. And he was right on my heels, because he didn't want me to get too far away from him.

There was just a little light, like I've said. I was between him and her. He was right behind me, watching me instead of anything else, and we went into the kitchen and I stepped aside quickly.

He almost stepped on her stomach. I guess his foot did touch it for a split second.

He pulled it back, staring down at her like his eyes were steel and she was a magnet. He tried to tug them away, and they'd just roll, going all-white in his head, and finally he got them away.

He looked at me and his lips shook as though he'd been playing a juice-harp, and he said:

"Yeeeeeeee!"

It was a hell of a funny sound, like a siren with a slippy chain that can't quite get started. "Yeeeeee!" he said. "Yeeeeee!" It sounded funny as hell, and he looked funny as hell.

Did you ever see one of these two-bit jazz singers? You know, trying to put something across with their bodies that they haven't got the voice to do? They lean back from the waist a little with their heads hanging forward and their hands held up about even with their ribs and swinging limp. And they sort of wobble and roll on their hips.

That's the way he looked, and he kept making that damned funny noise, his lips quivering ninety to the minute and his eyes rolling all-white.

I laughed and laughed, he looked and sounded so funny I couldn't help it. Then, I remembered what he'd done and I stopped laughing, and got mad—sore all over.

"You son-of-a-bitch," I said. "I was going to marry that poor little girl. We were going to elope and she caught you going through the house and you tried to . . ."

I stopped, because he hadn't done it at all. But he *could* have done it. He could've done it just as easy as not. The son-of-a-bitch could have, but he was just like everyone else. He was too nicey-nice and pretendsy to do anything really hard. But he'd stand back and crack the whip over me, keep moving around me every way I turned so that I couldn't get away no matter what I did, and it was always now-don't-you-do-nothin'-bud; but they kept cracking that old whip all the time they were sayin' it. And they— he'd done it all right; and I wasn't going to take the blame. I could be just as tricky and pretendsy as they were.

I could . . .

I went blind ma—angry seeing him so pretendsy shocked, "Yeeing!" and shivering and doing that screwy dance with his hands—hell, he hadn't had to watch *her* hands!—and white-rolling his eyes. What right did he have to act like that? I was the one that should have been acting that way, but, oh, no, I couldn't. That was their—his right to act that way, and I had to hold in and do all the dirty work.

I was as mad as all hell.

I snatched the butcher knife from under the newspaper, and made for him.

And my foot slipped where she'd been lying.

I went sprawling, almost knocking him over backwards if he hadn't moved, and the knife flew out of my hands.

I couldn't have moved a finger for a minute. I was laid out flat, helpless, without any weapon. And I could have maybe rolled a little and put my arms around her, and we'd have been together like we'd always been.

But do you think he'd do it? Do you think he'd pick up that knife and use it, just a little thing like that that wouldn't have been a bit of trouble? Oh, hell, no, oh, God, no, oh, Christ and Mary and all the Saints . . . ?

No.

All he could do was beat it, just like they always did.

I grabbed up the knife and took off after the heartless son-of-a-bitch.

He was out to the street sidewalk by the time I got to the front door; the dirty bastard had sneaked a head start on me. When I got out to the walk, he was better'n a half-block away, heading toward the center of town. I took after him as fast as I could go.

That wasn't very fast on account of the boots. I've seen plenty of men out here that never walked fifty miles altogether in their lives. But he wasn't moving very fast either. He was sort of skipping, jerky, rather than running or walking. He was skipping and tossing his head, and his hair was flying. And he still had his elbows held in at his sides, with his hands doing that funny floppy dance, and he kept saying—it was louder now—that old siren was warming up—he kept saying, kind of screaming:

"Yeeeee! Yeeeeee! Yeeeeeeeeee . . . !"

He was skipping and flopping his hands and tossing his head like one of those holy roller preachers at a brushwood's revival meeting. "Yeeeing!" and gone-to-Jesus and all you miserable sinners get right with Gawd like I went and done.

The dirty son-of-a-bitch! How low down can you get?

"MUR-DER!" I yelled. "Stop him, stop him! He killed Amy Stanton! MUR-DER . . . !"

I yelled at the top of my lungs and I kept yelling. And windows started banging up and doors slammed. And people ran down off their porches. And that snapped him out of that crap—some of it.

He skipped out into the middle of the street, and started moving faster. But I moved faster, too, because it was still dirt in this block, just one short of the business district, and boots are meant for dirt.

He saw that I was gaining a little on him, and he tried to come out of that floppy skippy stuff, but it didn't look like he could quite make it. Maybe he was using too much steam with that "Yeeeeing!"

"MURDER!" I yelled. "MUR-DER! Stop him! He killed Amy Stanton . . . !"

And everything was happening awful fast. It just sounds like it was a long time, because I'm not leaving out anything. I'm trying to tell you exactly how it was, so's you'll be sure to understand.

Looking up ahead, into the business district, it looked like a whole army of automobiles was bearing down on us. Then, suddenly, it was like a big plow had come down the street, pushing all those cars into the curb.

That's the way people are here in this section. That's the way they get. You don't see them rushing into the middle of a commotion to find out what's happening. There's men that are paid to do that and they do it prompt, without any fuss or feathers. And the folks know that no one's going to feel sorry for 'em if they get in the way of a gun or a bullet.

"Yeeeeee! Yeeeeee! Yeeeeeeeeeeeeeee!" he screamed, skipping and flopping.

"MUR-DER! He killed Amy Stanton. . . ."

And up ahead a little old roadster swung crossways with the intersection and stopped, and Jeff Plummer climbed out.

He reached down on the floor and took out a Winchester. Taking his time, easy-like. He leaned back against the fender, one boot heel hooked through the wheel spokes, and brought the gun up to his shoulder.

"Halt!" he called.

He called out the one time and then he fired, because the bum had started to skip toward the side of the street; and a man sure ought to know better than that.

The bum stumbled and went down, grabbing at his knee. But he got up again and he was still jerking and flopping his hands, and it looked like he was reaching into his clothes. And a man *really* hadn't ought to do that. He hadn't even ought to look anything like that.

Jeff fired three times, shifting his aim easy-like with each shot, and the bum was dropping with the first one, but all three got him. By the time he hit the dirt he didn't have much left in the way of a head.

I fell down on top of him and began beating him, and they had their hands full dragging me off. I babbled out the story—how I'd been upstairs getting ready and I'd heard some commotion but I hadn't thought much of it. And—

And I didn't have to tell it too good. They all seemed to understand how it was.

A doctor pushed through the crowd, Dr. Zweilman, and he gave me a shot in the arm; and then they took me home.

20

I woke up a little after nine the next morning.

My mouth was sticky and my throat dry from the morphine—I don't know why he hadn't used hyoscin like any damned fool should have—and all I could think of right then was how thirsty I was.

I stood in the bathroom, gulping down glass after glass of water, and pretty soon it began to bounce on me. (I'm telling you almost *anything* is better than morphine.) But after a while it stopped. I drank a couple glasses more, and they stayed down. And I scrubbed my face in hot and cold water, and combed my hair.

Then I went back and sat down on the bed, wondering who'd undressed me; and all at once it hit me. Not about her. I wouldn't think about that. But—well, this.

I shouldn't have been alone. Your friends don't leave you alone at a time like that. I'd lost the girl I was going to marry, and I'd been through a terrible experience. And they'd left me alone. There wasn't anyone around to comfort me, or wait on me or just sit and shake their heads and say it was God's will and she was happy, and

I—a man that's been through something like that needs those things. He needs all the help and comfort he can get, and I've never held back when one of my friends was bereaved. Why, hell, I—a man isn't himself when one of these disasters strikes. He might do something to himself, and the least people can do is have a nurse around. And . . .

But there wasn't any nurse around. I got up and looked through the other bedrooms, just to make sure.

And I wasn't doing anything to myself. They'd never done anything for me, and I wasn't doing anything for them.

I went downstairs and . . . and the kitchen had been cleaned up. There was no one there but me. I started to make some coffee, and then I thought I heard someone out in front, someone cough. And I was so all-fired glad I felt the tears come to my eyes. I turned off the coffee and went to the front door and opened it.

Jeff Plummer was sitting on the steps.

He was sitting sideways, his back to a porch post. He slanted a glance at me, then let his eyes go straight again, without turning his head.

"Gosh, Jeff," I said. "How long you been out here? Why didn't you knock?"

"Been here quite a spell," he said. And he fingered a stick of gum from his shirt pocket and began to unwrap it. "Yes, sir, I been here quite a spell."

"Well, come on in! I was just—"

"Kinda like it where I am," he said. "Air smells real good. Been smellin' real good, anyways."

He put the gum in his mouth. He folded the wrapper into a neat little square and tucked in back into his pocket.

"Yes, sir," he said, "it's been smellin' real good, and that's a fact."

I felt like I was nailed there in the doorway. I had to stand there and wait, watch his jaws move on that gum, look at him not looking at me. Never looking at me.

"Has there . . . hasn't anyone been—?"

"Told 'em you wasn't up to it," he said. "Told 'em you was all broke up about Bob Maples."

"Well, I—*Bob?*"

"Shot hisself around midnight last night. Yes, sir, pore ol' Bob killed hisself, and I reckon he had to. I reckon I know just how he felt."

And he still didn't look at me.

I closed the door.

I leaned against it, my eyes aching, my head pounding; and I ticked them off with the pounding that reached from my head to my heart . . . Joyce, Elmer, Johnnie Pappas, Amy, the . . . Him, Bob Maples. . . . But he hadn't known anything! He couldn't have known, had any real proof. He'd just jumped to conclusions like they were jumping. He couldn't wait for me to explain like, hell, I'd've been glad to do. Hadn't I always been glad to explain? But he couldn't wait; he'd made up his mind without any proof, like they'd made up theirs.

Just because I'd been around when a few people got killed, just because I happened to be around . . .

They couldn't know anything, because I was the only one who could tell 'em—show 'em—and I never had.

And I sure as hell wasn't going to.

Actually, well, logically, and you can't do away with logic, there *wasn't* anything. Existence and proof are inseparables. You have to have the second to have the first.

I held onto that thought, and I fixed myself a nice big breakfast. But I couldn't eat but a little bit. That darned morphine had taken all my appetite, just like it always does. About all I could get down was part of a piece of toast and two-three cups of coffee.

I went back upstairs and lighted a cigar, and stretched out on the bed. I—a man that'd been through what I had belonged in bed.

About a quarter of eleven, I heard the front door open and close, but I stayed right where I was. I still stayed there, stretched out on the bed, smoking, when Howard Hendricks and Jeff Plummer came in.

Howard gave me a curt nod, and drew up a straight chair near the bed. Jeff sat down, sort of out of the way, in an easy chair. Howard could hardly hold himself in, but he was sure trying. He tried. He did the best he could to be stern and sorrowful, and to hold his voice steady.

"Lou," he said, "we—I'm not at all satisfied. Last night's events—these recent events—I don't like them a bit, Lou."

"Well," I said, "that's natural enough. Don't hardly see how you could like 'em. I know I sure don't."

"You know what I mean!"

"Why, sure, I do. I know just how—"

"Now, this alleged robber-rapist—this poor devil you'd have us believe was a robber and rapist. We happen to know he was nothing of the kind! He was a pipeline worker. He had a pocket full of wages. And—and yes, we know he wasn't drunk because he'd just had a big steak dinner! He wouldn't have had the slightest reason to be in this house, so Miss Stanton couldn't have—"

"Are you saying he wasn't here, Howard?" I said. "That should be mighty easy to prove."

"Well—he wasn't prowling, that's a certainty! If—"

"Why is it?" I said. "If he wasn't prowling, what was he doing?"

His eyes began to glitter. "Never mind! Let that go for a minute! But I'll tell you this much. If you think you can get away with planting that money on him and making it look like—"

"What money?" I said. "I thought you said it was his wages?"

You see? The guy didn't have any sense. Otherwise, he'd have waited for me to mention that marked money.

"The money you stole from Elmer Conway! The money you took the night you killed him and that woman!"

"Now, wait a minute, wait a minute," I frowned. "Let's take one thing at a time. Let's take the woman. Why would I kill her?"

"Because—well—because you'd killed Elmer and you had to shut her up."

"But why would I kill Elmer? I'd known him all my life. If I'd wanted to do him any harm, I'd sure had plenty of chances."

"You know—" He stopped abruptly.

"Yeah?" I said, puzzled. "Why would I kill Elmer, Howard?"

And he couldn't say, of course. Chester Conway had given him his orders about that.

"You killed him all right," he said, his face reddening. "You killed her. You hanged Johnnie Pappas."

"You're sure not making much sense, Howard." I shook my head. "You plumb insisted on me talking to Johnnie because you knew how much I liked him and how much he liked me. Now you're saying I killed him."

"You had to kill him to protect yourself! You'd given him that marked twenty-dollar bill!"

"Now you really ain't making sense," I said. "Let's see; there was five hundred dollars missing, wasn't there? You claiming that I killed Elmer and that woman for five hundred dollars? Is that what you're saying, Howard?"

"I'm saying that—that—goddammit, Johnnie wasn't anywhere near the scene of the murders! He was stealing tires at the time they were committed!"

"Is that a fact?" I drawled. "Someone see him, Howard?"

"Yes! I mean, well—uh—"

See what I mean. Shrapnel.

"Let's say that Johnnie didn't do those killings," I said. "And you know it was mighty hard for me to believe that he had, Howard. I said so right along. I always did think he was just scared and kind of out of his mind when he hanged himself. I'd been his only friend, and now it sort of seemed like I didn't believe in him anymore an'—"

"His friend! Jesus!"

"So I reckon he didn't do it, after all. Poor little Amy was killed in pretty much the same way that other woman was. And this man—you say he had a big part of the missing money on him. Five hundred dollars would seem like a lot of money to a man like that, an' seeing that the two killings were so much alike . . ."

I let my voice trail off, smiling at him; and his mouth opened and went shut again.

Shrapnel. That's all he had.

"You've got it all figured out, haven't you?" he said, softly. "Four—five murders; six counting poor Bob Maples who staked everything he had on you, and you sit there explaining and smiling. You aren't bothered a bit. How can you do it, Ford? How can—"

I shrugged. "Somebody has to keep their heads, and it sure looks like you can't. You got some more questions, Howard?"

"Yes," he nodded slowly. "I've got one. How did Miss Stanton get those bruises on her body? Old bruises, not made last night. The same kind of bruises we found on the body of the Lakeland woman. How did she get them, Ford?"

Shrap—

"Bruises?" I said. "Gosh, you got me there, Howard. How would I know?"

"H-how"—he sputtered—"how would you know?"

"Yeah?" I said, puzzled. "How?"

"Why, goddam you! You'd been screwing that gal for years! You—"

"Don't say that," I said.

"No," said Jeff Plummer, "don't say that."

"But"—Howard turned on him, then turned back to

me. "All right, I won't say it! I don't need to say it. That girl had never gone with anyone but you, and only you could have done that to her! You'd been beating on her just like you'd beaten on that whore!"

I laughed, sort of sadly. "And Amy just took it huh, Howard? I bruised her up, and she went right ahead seeing me? She got all ready to marry me? That wouldn't make sense with any woman, and it makes no sense minus about Amy. You sure wouldn't say a thing like that if you'd known Amy Stanton."

He shook his head, staring, like I was some kind of curiosity. That old shrapnel wasn't doing a thing for him.

"Now, maybe Amy did pick up a bruise here and there," I went on. "She had all sorts of work to do, keepin' house and teaching school, and everything there was to be done. It'd been mighty strange if she didn't bang herself up a little, now and—"

"That's not what I mean. You know that's not what I mean."

"—but if you're thinking I did it, and that she put up with it, you're way off base. You sure didn't know Amy Stanton."

"Maybe," he said, "you didn't know her."

"Me? But you just got through sayin' we'd gone together for years—"

"I—" He hesitated, frowning. "I don't know. It isn't all clear to me, and I won't pretend that it is. But I don't think you knew her. Not as well as . . ."

"Yeah?" I said.

He reached into his inside coat pocket, and brought out

a square blue envelope. He opened it and removed one of those double sheets of stationery. I could see it was written on both sides, four pages in all. And I recognized that small neat handwriting.

Howard looked up from the paper, and caught my eye.

"This was in her purse." *Her purse.* "She'd written it at home and was planning, apparently, to give it to you after you were out of Central City. As a matter of fact"—he glanced down at the letter—"she intended to have you stop at a restaurant up the road, and have you read it while she was in the restroom. Now, it begins, ' Lou Darling . . .' "

"Let me have it," I said.

"I'll read—"

"It's his letter," said Jeff. "Let him have it."

"Very well." Howard shrugged; and he tossed me the letter. And I knew he'd planned on having me read it all along. He wanted me to read it while he sat back and watched.

I looked down at the thick double page, holding my eyes on it:

Lou, Darling:

Now you know why I had you stop here, and why I've excused myself from the table. It was to allow you to read this, the things I couldn't somehow otherwise say to you. Please, please read carefully, darling. I'll give you plenty of time. And if I sound confused and rambling, please don't be angry with me. It's only because I love you so much, and I'm a little frightened and worried.

Darling, I wish I could tell you how happy you've made me these last few weeks. I wish I could be sure that you'd been even a tiny fraction as happy. Just a teensy-weensie bit as much. Sometimes I get the crazy, wonderful notion that you have been, that you were even as happy as I was (though I don't see how you could be!) and at others I tell myself . . . Oh, I don't know, Lou!

I suppose the trouble is that it all seemed to come about so suddenly. We'd gone on for years, and you seemed to be growing more and more indifferent; you seemed to keep drawing away from me and taking pleasure in making me follow. (Seemed, Lou; I don't say you did do it.) I'm not trying to excuse myself, darling. I only want to explain, to make you understand that I'm not going to behave that way any more. I'm not going to be sharp and demanding and scolding and . . . I may not be able to change all at once (oh, but I will, darling; I'll watch myself; I'll do it just as fast as I can) but if you'll just love me, Lou, just act like you love me, I'm sure—

Do you understand how I felt? Just a little? Do you see why I was that way, then, and why I won't be anymore? Everyone knew I was yours. Almost everyone. I wanted it to be that way; to have anyone else was unthinkable. But I couldn't have had anyone else if I'd wished to. I was yours. I'd always be yours if you dropped me. And it seemed, Lou, that you were slipping further and further away, still owning me yet not letting yourself belong to me. You were (it seemed, darling, seemed) leaving me with nothing—and knowing that you were doing it, knowing I was helpless—and apparently enjoying it. You avoided

me. *You made me chase you. You made me question you
and beg you, and—and then you'd act so innocent and
puzzled and . . . Forgive me, darling. I don't want to crit-
icize you ever, ever again. I only wanted you to understand, and I suppose only another woman could do that.*

*Lou, I want to ask you something, a few things, and I
want to beg you please, please, please not to take it the
wrong way. Are you—oh, don't be, darling—are you
afraid of me? Do you feel that you have to be nice to me?
There I won't say anything more, but you know what I
mean, as well as I do at least. And you will know . . .*

*I hope and pray I am wrong, darling. I do so hope. But
I'm afraid—are you in trouble? Is something weighing on
your mind? I don't want to ask you more than that, but
I do want you to believe that whatever it is, even if it's
what I—whatever it is, Lou, I'm on your side. I love you
(are you tired of my saying that?), and I know you. I
know you'd never knowingly do anything wrong, you just
couldn't, and I love you so much and . . . Let me help
you, darling. Whatever it is, whatever help you need. Even
if it should involve being separated for a while, a long
while, let's—let me help you. Because I'll wait for you,
however long—and it mightn't be long at all, it might be
just a question of—well, it will be all right, Lou, because
you wouldn't knowingly do anything. I know that and
everyone else knows it, and it will be all right. We'll make
it all right, you and I together. If you'll only tell me. If
you'll just let me help you.*

*Now. I asked you not to be afraid of me, but I know
how you've felt, how you used to feel, and I know that*

asking you or telling you might not be enough. That's
why I had you stop at this place, here at a bus stop. That's
why I'm giving you so much time. To prove to you that
you don't need to be afraid.

I hope that when I come back to the table, you'll still
be there. But if you aren't, darling, if you feel that you
can't . . . then just leave my bags inside the door. I have
money with me and I can get a job in some other town,
and—do that, Lou. If you feel that you must. I'll understand, and it'll be perfectly all right—honestly it will,
Lou—and . . .

Oh, darling, darling, darling, I love you so much. I've
always loved you and I always will, whatever happens. Always, darling. Always and always. Forever and forever.

Always and forever,
Amy

Well. WELL?

What are you going to do? What are you going to say?

What are you going to say when you're drowning in your own dung and they keep booting you back into it, when all the screams in hell wouldn't be as loud as you want to scream, when you're at the bottom of the pit and the whole world's at the top, when it has but one face, a face without eyes or ears, and yet it watches and listens. . . .

What are you going to do and say? Why, pardner, that's simple. It's easy as nailing your balls to a stump and falling off backwards. Snow again, pardner, and drift me hard, because that's an easy one.

You're gonna say, they can't keep a good man down. You're gonna say, a winner never quits and a quitter never wins. You're gonna smile, boy, you're gonna show 'em the ol' fightin' smile. And then you're gonna get out there an' hit 'em hard and fast and low, an'—an' Fight!"

Rah.

I folded the letter, and tossed it back to Howard.

"She was sure a talky little girl," I said. "Sweet but

awful talky. Seems like if she couldn't say it to you, she'd write it down for you."

Howard swallowed. "That—that's all you have to say?"

I lit a cigar, pretending like I hadn't heard him. Jeff Plummer's chair creaked. "I sure liked Miss Amy," he said. "All four of my younguns went to school to her, an' she was just as nice as if they'd had one of these oilmen for a daddy."

"Yes, sir," I said, "I reckon she really had her heart in her work."

I puffed on my cigar, and Jeff's chair creaked again, louder than the first time, and the hate in Howard's eyes seemed to lash out against me. He gulped like a man choking down puke.

"You fellows getting restless?" I said. "I sure appreciate you dropping in at a time like this, but I wouldn't want to keep you from anything important."

"You—y-you!"

"You starting to stutter, Howard? You ought to practice talking with a pebble in your mouth. Or maybe a piece of shrapnel."

"You dirty son-of-a-bitch! You—"

"Don't call me that," I said.

"No," said Jeff, "don't call him that. Don't never say anything about a man's mother."

"To hell with that crap! He—you"—he shook his fist at me—"you killed that little girl. She as good as says so!"

I laughed. "She wrote it down after I killed her, huh? That's quite a trick."

"You know what I mean. She knew you were going to kill her . . ."

"And she was going to marry me, anyway?"

"She knew you'd killed all those other people!"

"Yeah? Funny she didn't mention it."

"She did mention it! She—"

"Don't recall seeing anything like that. Don't see that she said anything much. Just a lot of woman-worry talk."

"You killed Joyce Lakeland and Elmer Conway and Johnnie Pappas and—"

"President McKinley?"

He sagged back in his chair, breathing hard. "You killed them, Ford. You killed them."

"Why don't you arrest me, then? What are you waiting on?"

"Don't worry," he nodded grimly. "Don't you worry. I'm not waiting much longer."

"And I'm not either," I said.

"What do you mean?"

"I mean you and your courthouse gang are doing spite work. You're pouring it on me because Conway says to, just why I can't figure out. You haven't got a shred of proof but you've tried to smear me—"

"Now, wait a minute! We haven't—"

"You've tried to; you had Jeff out here this morning chasing visitors away. You'd do it, but you can't because you haven't got a shred of proof and people know me too well. You know you can't get a conviction, so you try to ruin my reputation. And with Conway backing you up you may manage it in time. You'll manage it if you have the time, and I guess I can't stop you. But I'm not going to sit back and take it. I'm leaving town, Howard."

"Oh, no you're not. I'm warning you here and now, Ford, don't you even attempt to leave."

"Who's going to stop me?"

"I am."

"On what grounds?"

"Mur—suspicion of murder."

"But who suspects me, Howard, and why? The Stantons? I reckon not. Mike Pappas? Huh-uh. Chester Conway? Well, I've got kind of a funny feeling about Conway, Howard. I've got a feeling that he's going to stay in the background, he's not going to do or say a thing, no matter how bad you need him."

"I see," he said. "I see."

"You see that opening there behind you?" I said. "Well, that's a door, Howard, in case you were wonderin', and I can't think of a thing to keep you and Mister Plummer from walking through it."

"We're walking through it," said Jeff, "and so are you."

"Huh-uh," I said, "no I ain't. I sure ain't aimin' to do nothing like that, Mister Plummer. And that's a fact."

Howard kept his seat. His face looked like a blob of reddish dough, but he shook his head at Jeff and kept his seat. Howard was really trying hard.

"I—it's to your own interest as well as ours to get this settled, Ford. I'm asking you to place yourself—to remain available until—"

"You mean you want me to cooperate with you?" I said.

"Yes."

"That door," I said. "I wish you'd close it real careful. I'm suffering from shock, and I might have a relapse."

Howard's mouth twisted and opened, and snapped shut. He sighed and reached for his hat.

"I sure liked Bob Maples," said Jeff. "I sure liked that little Miss Amy."

"Sure enough?" I said, "Is that a fact?"

I laid my cigar down on an ashtray, leaned back on the pillow and closed my eyes. A chair creaked and squeaked real loud, and I heard Howard say, "Now Jeff"—and there was a sound like he'd sort of stumbled.

I opened my eyes again. Jeff Plummer was standing over me.

He was smiling down at me with his lips and there was a .45 in his hand, and the hammer was thumbed back.

"You right sure you ain't coming with us?" he said. "You don't reckon you could change your mind?"

The way he sounded I knew he hoped I wouldn't change it. He was just begging, waiting for me to say no. And I reckoned I wouldn't say all of even a short word like that before I was past saying anything.

I got up and began to dress.

22

If I'd known that Rothman's lawyer friend, Billy Boy Walker, was tied up in the East and was having trouble getting away, I might have felt different. I might have cracked up right off. But, on the other hand, I don't think I would have. I had a feeling that I was speeding fast down a one-way trail, that I was almost to the place I had to get to. I was almost there and moving fast, so why hop off and try to run ahead? It wouldn't have made a particle of sense, and you know I don't do things that don't make sense. You know it or you will know it.

That first day and that night, I spent in one of the "quiet" cells, but the next morning they put me on ice, down in the cooler where I'd—where Johnnie Pappas had died. They—

How's that? Well, sure they can do it to you. They can do anything they're big enough to do and you're little enough to take. They don't book you. No one knows where you are, and you've got no one on the outside that can get you out. It's not legal, but I found out long ago that the place where the law is apt to be abused most is right around a courthouse.

Yeah, they can do it all right.

So I was saying. I spent the first day and night in one of the quiet cells, and most of the time I was trying to kid myself. I couldn't face up to the truth yet, so I tried to play like there was a way around it. You know. Those kid games?

You've done something pretty bad or you want something bad, and you think, well, if I can just do such and such I can fix it. If I can count down from a thousand backwards by three and a third or recite the Gettysburg address in pig-latin while I'm touching my little toes with my big ones, everything will be all right.

I'd play those games and their kin-kind, doing real impossible things in my imagination. I'd trot all the way from Central City to San Angelo without stopping. Or they'd grease the pipeline across the Pecos River, and I'd hop across it on one foot with my eyes blindfolded and an anvil around my neck. I'd really get to sweating and panting sometimes. My feet'd be all achy and blistered from pounding that San Angelo Highway, and that old anvil would keep swinging and dragging at me, trying to pull me off into the Pecos; and finally I'd win through, just plumb worn out. And—and I'd have to do something still harder.

Well, then they moved me down into the cooler where Johnnie Pappas had died, and pretty soon I saw why they hadn't put me there right away. They'd had a little work to do on it first. I don't know just how they'd rigged the stunt—only that that unused light-socket in the ceiling was part of it. But I was stretched out on the bunk, fixing to shinny up the water tower without using my hands, when all at once I heard Johnnie's voice:

"Hello, you lovely people. I'm certainly having a fine time and I wish you were here. See you soon."

Yes, it was Johnnie, speaking in that sharp smart-alecky way he used a lot. I jumped up from the bunk and started turning around and looking up and down and sideways. And here his voice came again:

"Hello, you lovely people. I'm certainly having a fine time and I wish you were here. See you soon."

He kept saying the same thing over and over, about fifteen seconds between times, and, hell, as soon as I had a couple minutes to think, I knew what it was all about. It was one of those little four-bit voice recordings, like you've just about got time to sneeze on before it's used up. Johnnie'd sent it to his folks the time he visited the Dallas Fair. He'd mentioned it to me when he told me about the trip—and I'd remembered because I liked Johnnie and would remember. He'd mentioned it, apologizing for not sending me some word. But he'd lost all his dough in some kind of wheel game and had to hitchhike back to Central City.

"Hello, you lovely people . . ."

I wondered what kind of story they'd given the Greek, because I was pretty sure he wouldn't have let 'em have it if he'd known what it was going to be used for. He knew how I felt about Johnnie and how Johnnie'd felt about me.

They kept playing that record over and over, from maybe five in the morning until midnight; I don't know just what the hours were because they'd taken away my watch. It didn't even stop when they brought me food and water twice a day.

I'd lie and listen to it, or sit and listen. And every once in a while, when I could remember to do it, I'd jump up and pace around the cell. I'd pretend like it was bothering the hell out of me, which of course it didn't at all. Why would it? But I wanted 'em to think it did, so they wouldn't turn it off. And I guess I must have pretended pretty good, because they played it for three days and part of a fourth. Until it wore out, I reckon.

After that there wasn't much but silence, nothing but those faraway sounds like the factory whistles which weren't any real company for a man.

They'd taken away my cigars and matches, of course, and I fidgeted around quite a bit the first day, thinking I wanted a smoke. Yeah, *thinking,* because I didn't actually want one. I'd been smoking cigars for—well—around eleven years; ever since my eighteenth birthday when Dad had said I was getting to be a man, so he hoped I'd act like one and smoke cigars and not go around with a coffin-nail in my mouth. So I'd smoked cigars, from then on, never admitting to myself that I didn't like them. But now I could admit it. I had to, and I did.

When life attains a crisis, man's focus narrows. *Nice lines, huh? I could talk that way all the time if I wanted to.* The world becomes a stage of immediate concern, swept free of illusion. *I used to could talk that way all the time.*

No one had pushed me around or even tried to question me since the morning they'd locked me up. No one, at all. And I'd tried to tell myself that that was a good sign. They didn't have any evidence; I'd got their goats, so they'd put me on ice, just like they'd done with plenty of other guys. And pretty soon they'd simmer down and let me go of their own accord, or Billy Boy Walker'd show up and they'd have to let me out . . . that's what I'd told myself and it made sense—all my reasoning does. But it was top-of-the-cliff sense, not the kind you make when you're down near the tag-end of the rope.

They hadn't tried to beat the truth out of me or talk it out of me for a couple of reasons. First of all, they were pretty sure it wouldn't do any good. You can't stamp on a man's corns when he's got his feet cut off. Second—the second reason was—they didn't think they had to.

They *had* evidence.

They'd had it right from the beginning.

Why hadn't they sprung it on me? Well, there were a couple of reasons behind that, too. For one thing, they weren't sure that it was evidence because they weren't sure about me. I'd thrown them off the track with Johnnie Pappas. For another thing, they *couldn't* use it—it wasn't in shape to be used.

But now they were sure of what I'd done, though they probably weren't too clear as to why I'd done it. And that evidence would be ready to be used before long. And I didn't reckon they'd let go of me until it was ready. Conway was determined to get me, and they'd gone too far to back down.

I thought back to the day Bob Maples and I had gone to Fort Worth, and how Conway hadn't invited us on the trip but had got busy ordering us around the minute we'd landed. You see? What could be clearer? He'd tipped his hand on me right there.

Then, Bob had come back to the hotel, and he was all upset about something Conway had said to him, ordered him to do. And he wouldn't tell me what it was. He just talked on and on about how long he'd known me and what a swell guy I was, and . . . Hell, don't you see? Don't you get it?

I'd let it go by me because I had to. I couldn't let myself face the facts. But I reckon you've known the truth all along.

Then, I'd brought Bob home on the train and he'd been babbling drunk, and he'd gotten sore about some of my kidding. So he'd snapped back at me, giving me a tip on where I stood at the same time. He'd said—what was it?— *"It's always lightest just before the dark. . . ."*

He'd been sore and drunk so he'd come out with that. He was telling me in so many words that I might not be sitting nearly as pretty as I thought I was. And he was certainly right about that—but I think he'd got his words twisted a little. He was saying 'em to be sarcastic, but they happen to be the truth. At least it seemed so to me.

It *is* lightest just before the dark. Whatever a man is up against, it makes him feel better to know that he *is* up against it. That's the way it seemed to me, anyhow, and I ought to know.

Once I'd admitted the truth about that piece of evidence, it was easy to admit other things. I could stop inventing reasons for what I'd done, stop believing in the reasons I'd invented, and see the truth. And it sure wasn't hard to see. When you're climbing up a cliff or just holding on for dear life, you keep your eyes closed. You know you'll get dizzy and fall if you don't. But after you fall down to the bottom, you open 'em again. And you can see just where you started from, and trace every foot of your trail up that cliff.

Mine had started back with the housekeeper; with Dad finding out about us. All kids pull some pretty sorry stunts, particularly if an older person edges 'em along, so it hadn't needed to mean a thing. But Dad had made it mean something. I'd been made to feel that I'd done something that couldn't ever be forgiven—that would always lie between him and me, the only kin I had. And there wasn't anything I could do or say that would change things. I had a burden of fear and shame put on me that I could never get shed of.

She was gone, and I couldn't strike back at her, yes, kill her, for what I'd been made to feel she'd done to me. But that was all right. She was the first woman I'd ever known; she *was* woman to me; and all womankind bore her face. So I could strike back at any of them, any female, the ones it would be safest to strike at, and it would be the same as striking at her. And I did that, I started striking out . . . and Mike Dean took the blame.

Dad tightened the reins on me after that. I could hardly be out of his sight an hour without his checking up on me. So years passed and I didn't strike out again, and I was able to distinguish between women and *the* woman. Dad slacked off on the reins a little; I seemed to be normal. But every now and then I'd catch myself in that dead-pan kidding, trying to ease the terrific pressure that was building up inside of me. And even without that I knew—though I wouldn't recognize the fact—that I wasn't all right.

If I could have got away somewhere, where I wouldn't have been constantly reminded of what had happened and I'd had something I wanted to do—something to occupy my mind—it might have been different. But I couldn't get away, and there wasn't anything here I wanted to do. So nothing had changed; I was still looking for *her*. And any woman who'd done what she had would be *her*.

I'd kept pushing Amy away from me down through the years, not because I didn't love her but because I did. I was afraid of what might happen between us. I was afraid of what I'd do . . . what I finally did.

I could admit, now, that I'd never had any real cause to think that Amy would make trouble for me. She had too much pride; she'd have hurt herself too much; and, anyway, she loved me.

I'd never had any real cause, either, to be afraid that Joyce would make trouble. She was too smart to try to, from what I'd seen of her. But if she had been sore enough to try—if she'd been mad enough so's she just didn't give a damn—she wouldn't have got anywhere. After all, she was just a whore and I was old family, quality; and she wouldn't have opened her mouth more than twice before she was run out of town.

No, I hadn't been afraid of her starting talk. I hadn't been afraid that if I kept on with her I'd lose control of myself. I'd never had any control even before I met her. No control—only luck. Because anyone who reminded me of the burden I carried, anyone who did what that first *her* had done, would get killed. . . .

Anyone. Amy. Joyce. Any woman who, even for a moment, became *her*.

I'd kill them.

I'd keep trying until I did kill them.

Elmer Conway had had to suffer, too, on *her* account. Mike had taken the blame for me, and then he'd been killed. So, along with the burden, I had a terrible debt to him that I couldn't pay. I could never repay him for what he'd done for me. The only thing I could do was what I did . . . try to settle the score with Chester Conway.

That was my main reason for killing Elmer, but it wasn't the only one. The Conways were part of the circle, the town, that ringed me in; the smug ones, the hypocrites, the holier-than-thou guys—all the stinkers I had to face day in and day out. I had to grin and smile and be pleasant to them; and maybe there are people like that everywhere, but when you can't get away from them, when they keep pushing themselves at you, and you can't get away, never, never, get away . . .

Well.

The bum. The few others I'd struck out at. I don't know—I'm not really sure about them.

They were all people who didn't have to stay here. People who took what was handed them because they didn't have enough pride or guts to strike back. So maybe that was it. Maybe I think that the guy who won't fight when he can and should deserves the worst you can toss at him.

Maybe. I'm not sure of all the details. All I can do is give you the general picture; and not even the experts could do more than that.

I've read a lot of stuff by a guy—name of Kraepelin, I believe—and I can't remember all of it, of course, or even the gist of all of it. But I remember the high points of some, the most important stuff, and I think it goes something like this:

". . . difficult to study because so seldom detected. The condition usually begins around the period of puberty, and is often precipitated by a severe shock. The subject suffers from strong feelings of guilt . . . combined with a sense of frustration and persecution . . . which increase as he grows older; yet there are rarely if ever any surface signs of . . . disturbance. On the contrary, his behavior appears to be entirely logical. He reasons soundly, even shrewdly. He is completely aware of what he does and why he does it. . . ."

That was written about a disease, or a condition, rather, called dementia praecox. Schizophrenia, paranoid type. Acute, recurrent, advanced.

Incurable.

It was written, you might say, about—

But I reckon you know, don't you?

23

I was in jail eight days, but no one questioned me and they didn't pull any more stunts like that voice recording. I kind of looked for them to do the last because they couldn't be positive about that piece of evidence they had—about my reaction to it, that is. They weren't certain that it would make me put the finger on myself. And even if they had been certain, I knew they'd a lot rather I cracked up and confessed of my own accord. If I did that they could probably send me to the chair. The other way—if they used their evidence—they couldn't.

But I reckon they weren't set up right at the jail for any more stunts or maybe they couldn't get ahold of the equipment they needed. At any rate, they didn't pull any more. And on the eighth day, around eleven o'clock at night, they transferred me to the insane asylum.

They put me in a pretty good room—better'n any I'd seen the time I'd had to take a poor guy there years before—and left me alone. But I took one look around and I knew I was being watched through those little slots high up on the walls. They wouldn't have left me in a room with cigarette tobacco and matches and a drinking glass and water pitcher unless someone was watching me.

I wondered how far they'd let me go if I started to cut my throat or wrap myself in a sheet and set fire to it, but I didn't wonder very long. It was late, and I was pretty well worn out after sleeping on that bunk in the cooler. I smoked a couple of hand-rolled cigarettes, putting the butts out real careful. Then with the lights still burning—there wasn't any switch for me to turn 'em off—I stretched out on the bed and went to sleep.

About seven in the morning, a husky-looking nurse came in with a couple of young guys in white jackets. And she took my temperature and pulse while they stood and waited. Then, she left and the two attendants took me down the hall to a shower room, and watched while I took a bath. They didn't act particularly tough or unpleasant, but they didn't say a word more than they needed to. I didn't say anything.

I finished my shower and put my short-tailed nightgown back on. We went back to my room, and one of 'em made up my bed while the other went after my breakfast. The scrambled eggs tasted pretty flat, and it didn't help my appetite any to have them cleaning up the room, emptying the enamel night-can and so on. But I ate almost everything and drank all of the weak lukewarm coffee. They were through cleaning by the time I'd finished. They left, locking me in again.

I smoked a hand-rolled cigarette, and it tasted good.

I wondered—no I didn't, either. I didn't need to wonder what it would be like to spend your whole life like this.

Not a tenth as good as this probably, because I was something pretty special right now. Right now I was a hideout; I'd been kidnapped, actually. And there was always a chance that there'd be a hell of a stink raised. But if that hadn't been the case, if I'd been committed—well, I'd still be something special, in a different way. I'd be worse off than anyone in the place.

Conway would see to that, even if Doc Bony-face didn't have a special sort of interest in me.

I'd kind of figured that the Doc might show up with his hard-rubber playthings, but I guess he had just enough sense to know that he was out of his class. Plenty of pretty smart psychiatrists have been fooled by guys like me, and you can't really fault 'em for it. There's just not much they can put their hands on, know what I mean?

We might have the disease, the condition; or we might just be cold-blooded and smart as hell; or we might be innocent of what we're supposed to have done. We might be any one of those three things, because the symptoms we show would fit any one of the three.

So Bony-face didn't give me any trouble. No one did. The nurse checked on me night and morning, and the two attendants carried on with pretty much the same routine. Bringing my meals, taking me to the shower, cleaning up the room. The second day, and every other day after that, they let me shave with a safety razor while they stood by and watched.

I thought about Rothman and Billy Boy Walker, just thought, wondered, without worrying any. Because, hell,

I didn't have anything to worry about, and they were probably doing enough worrying for all three of us. But—

But I'm getting ahead of myself.

They, Conway and the others, still weren't positive about that piece of evidence they had; and, like I say, they preferred to have me crack up and confess. So, on the evening of my second night in the asylum, there came the stunt.

I was lying on my side in bed, smoking a cigarette, when the lights dimmed way down, down to almost nothing. Then, there was a click and a flash up above me, and Amy Stanton stood looking at me from the far wall of the room.

Oh, sure, it was a picture; one that had been made into a glass slide. I didn't need to do any figuring at all to know that they were using a slide projector to throw her picture against the wall. She was coming down the walk of her house, smiling, but looking kind of fussed like I'd seen her so many times. I could almost hear her saying, *"Well, you finally got here, did you?"* And I knew it was just a picture, but it looked so real, it seemed so real, that I answered her back in my mind. *"Kinda looks that way, don't it?"*

I guess they'd got a whole album of her pictures. Which wouldn't have been any trouble, since the old folks, the Stantons, were awfully innocent and accommodating and not given to asking questions. Anyway, after that first picture, which was a pretty recent one, there was one taken when she was about fifteen years old. And they worked up through the years from that.

They . . . I saw her the day she graduated from high school, she was sixteen that spring, wearing one of those white lacy dresses and flat-heeled slippers, and standing real stiff with her arms held close to her sides.

I saw her sitting on her front steps, laughing in spite of herself . . . *it always seemed hard for Amy to laugh* . . . because that old dog of theirs was trying to lick her on the ear.

I saw her all dressed up, and looking kind of scared, the time she started off for teachers' college. I saw her the day she finished her two-year course, standing very straight with her hand on the back of a chair and trying to look older than she was.

I saw her—and I'd taken a lot of those pictures myself; it seemed just like yesterday—I saw her working in the garden, in a pair of old jeans; walking home from church and kind of frowning up at the little hat she'd made for herself; coming out of the grocery store with both arms around a big sack; sitting in the porch swing with an apple in her hand and a book in her lap.

I saw her with her dress pulled way up high—she'd just slid off the fence where I'd taken a snap of her—and she was bent over, trying to cover herself, and yelling at me, *"Don't you dare, Lou! Don't you dare, now!"* . . . She'd sure been mad about me taking that picture, but she'd saved it.

I saw her . . .

I tried to remember how many pictures there were, to figure out how long they would last. They were sure in a hell of a hurry to get through with them, it looked like to me. They were just racing through 'em, it seemed like. I'd just be starting to enjoy a picture, remembering when it was taken and how old Amy was at the time, when they'd flash it off and put on another one.

It was a pretty sorry way to act, the way I saw it. You know, it was as though she wasn't worth looking at; like, maybe they'd seen someone that was better to look at. And I'm not prejudiced or anything, but you wouldn't find a girl as pretty and well-built as Amy Stanton in a month of Sundays.

Aside from being a slight on Amy, it was damned stupid to rush through those pictures like they were doing . . . like they seemed to be doing. After all, the whole object of the show was to make me crack up, and how could I do it if they didn't even let me get a good look at her?

I wasn't going to crack up, of course; I felt stronger and better inside every time I saw her. But they didn't know that, and it doesn't excuse them. They were lying down on the job. They had a doggone ticklish job to do, and they were too lazy and stupid to do it right.

Well . . .

They'd started showing the pictures about eight-thirty, and they should have lasted until one or two in the morning. But they had to be in a hell of a hurry, so it was only around eleven when they came to the last one.

It was a picture I'd taken less than three weeks before, and they *did* leave it on long enough—well, not long enough, but they let me get a good look at it. She and I had fixed up a little lunch that evening, and eaten it over in Sam Houston Park. And I'd taken this picture just as she was stepping back into the car. She was looking over her shoulder at me, wide-eyed, smiling but sort of impatient. Saying:

"Can't you hurry a little, darling?"

Hurry?

"Well, I reckon so, honey. I'll sure try to."

"When, Lou? How soon will I see you, darling?"

"Well, now, honey. I—I . . ."

I was almost glad right then that the lights came back on. I never was real good at lying to Amy.

I got up and paced around the room. I went over by the wall where they'd flashed the pictures, and I rubbed my eyes with my fists and gave the wall a few pats and tugged my hair a little.

I put on a pretty good act, it seemed to me. Just good enough to let 'em think I was bothered, but not enough to mean anything at a sanity hearing.

The nurse and the two attendants didn't have any more to say than usual the next morning. It seemed to me, though, that they acted a little different, more watchful sort of. So I did a lot of frowning and staring down at the floor, and I only ate part of my breakfast.

I passed up most of my lunch and dinner, too, which wasn't much of a chore, hungry as I was. And I did everything else I could to put on just the right kind of act—not too strong, not too weak. But I was too anxious. I had to go and ask the nurse a question when she made the night check on me, and that spoiled everything.

"Will they be showing the pictures tonight?" I said, and I knew doggone well it was the wrong thing to do.

"What pictures? I don't know anything about pictures," she said.

"The pictures of my girl. You know. Will they show 'em, ma'am?"

She shook her head, a kind of mean glint in her eye. "You'll see. You'll find out, mister."

"Well, tell 'em not to do it so fast," I said. "When they do it so fast, I don't get to see her very good. I hardly get to look at her at all before she's gone."

She frowned. She shook her head, staring at me, like she hadn't heard me right. She edged away from the bed a little.

"You"—she swallowed—"you want to see those pictures?"

"Well—uh—I—"

"You *do* want to see them," she said slowly. "You want to see the pictures of the girl you—you—"

"Sure, I want to see 'em." I began to get sore. "Why shouldn't I want to see them? What's wrong with that? Why the hell wouldn't I want to see them?"

The attendants started to move toward me. I lowered my voice.

"I'm sorry," I said, "I don't want to cause any trouble. If you folks are too busy, maybe you could move the projector in here. I know how to run one, and I'd take good care of it."

That was a pretty bad night for me. There weren't any

pictures, and I was so hungry I couldn't go to sleep for hours. I was sure glad when morning came.

So, that was the end of their stunt, and they didn't try any others. I reckon they figured it was a waste of time. They just kept me from then on; just held me without me saying any more than I had to and them doing the same.

That went on for six days, and I was beginning to get puzzled. Because that evidence of theirs should have been about ready to use, by now, if it was ever going to be ready.

The seventh day rolled around, and I was really getting baffled. And, then, right after lunch, Billy Boy Walker showed up.

24

"Where is he?" he yelled. "What have you done with the poor man? Have you torn out his tongue? Have you roasted his poor broken body over slow fires? Where is he, I say?"

He was coming down the corridor, yelling at the top of his lungs; and I could hear several people scurrying along with him, trying to shush him up, but no one had ever had much luck at that and they didn't either. I'd never seen him in my life—just heard him a couple of times on the radio—but I knew it was him. I reckon I'd have known he'd come even if I hadn't heard him. You didn't have to see or hear Billy Boy Walker to know he was around. You could just kind of sense it.

They stopped in front of my door, and Billy Boy started beating on it like they didn't have a key and he was going to have to knock it down.

"Mr. Ford! My poor man!" he yelled; and, man, I'll bet they could hear him all the way into Central City. "Can you hear me? Have they punctured your eardrums? Are you too weak to cry out? Be brave, my poor fellow!"

He kept it up, beating on the door and yelling, and it sounds like it must've been funny but somehow it wasn't. Even to me, knowing that they hadn't done a thing to me, really, it didn't sound funny. I could almost believe that they *had* put me through the works.

They managed to get the door unlocked, and he came bounding in. And he looked as funny—he should have looked as funny as he should have sounded—but I didn't feel the slightest call to laugh. He was short and fat and pot-bellied; and a couple of buttons were off his shirt and his belly button was showing. He was wearing a baggy old black suit and red suspenders; and he had a big floppy black hat sitting kind of crooked on his head. Everything about him was sort of off-size and out-of-shape, as the saying is. But I couldn't see a thing to laugh about. Neither, apparently, could the nurse and the two attendants and old Doc Bony-face.

Billy Boy flung his arms around me and called me a "poor man" and patted me on the head. He had to reach up to do it; but he didn't seem to reach and it didn't seem funny.

He turned around, all at once, and grabbed the nurse by the arm. "Is this the woman, Mr. Ford? Did she beat you with chains? Fie! Fah! Abomination!" And he scrubbed his hand against his pants, glaring at her.

The attendants were helping me into my clothes, and they weren't losing any time about it. But you'd never have known it to hear Billy Boy. "Fiends!" he yelled. "Will your sadistic appetites never be satiated? Must you continue to stare and slaver over your handiwork? Will you not clothe this poor tortured flesh, this broken creature that was once a man built in God's own image?"

The nurse was spluttering and sputtering, her face a half-dozen different colors. The doc's bones were leaping like jumping-jacks. Billy Boy Walker snatched up the night-can, and shoved it under his nose. "You fed him from this, eh? I thought so! Bread and water, served in a slop jar! Shame, shame, fie! You did do it? Answer me, sirrah! You didn't do it? Fie, fah, paah! Perjurer, suborner! Answer, yes or no!"

The doc shook his head, and then nodded. He shook and nodded it at the same time. Billy Boy dropped the can to the floor, and took me by the arm. "Never mind your gold watch, Mr. Ford. Never mind the money and jewelry they have stolen. You have your clothes. Trust me to recover the rest—and more! Much, much more, Mr. Ford."

He pushed me out the door ahead of him, and then he turned around real slow and pointed around the room. "You," he said softly, pointing them out one by one. "You and you and you are through. This is the end for you. The end."

He looked them all in the eye, and no one said a word and none of them moved. He took me by the arm again, and we went down the corridor, and each of the three gates were open for us before we got to 'em.

He squeezed in behind the wheel of the car he'd rented in Central City. He started it up with a roar and a jerk, and we went speeding out through the main gate to the highway where two signs, facing in opposite directions, read:

WARNING! WARNING!
Hitchhikers May Be Escaped
LUNATICS!

He lifted himself in the seat, reached into his hip pocket, and pulled out a plug of tobacco. He offered it to me and I shook my head, and he took a big chew.

"Dirty habit," he said, in just a quiet conversational voice. "Got it young, though, and I reckon I'll keep it."

He spat out the window, wiped his chin with his hand, and wiped his hand on his pants. I found the makings I'd had at the asylum and started rolling a cigarette.

"About Joe Rothman," I said. "I didn't say anything about him, Mr. Walker."

"Why, I didn't think you had, Mr. Ford! It never occurred to me that you would," he said; and whether he meant it or not he sure sounded like it. "You know somethin', Mr. Ford? There wasn't a bit of sense in what I did back there."

"No," I said.

"No, sir, not a bit. I've been snorting and pawing up the earth around here for four days. Couldn't have fought harder getting Christ off the cross. And I reckon it was just habit like this chewing tobacco—I knew it but I kept right on chewing. I didn't get you free, Mr. Ford. I didn't have a thing to do with it. They *let* me have a writ. They *let* me know where you were. That's why you're here, Mr. Ford, instead of back there."

"I know," I said. "I figured it would be that way."

"You understand? They're not letting you go; they've gone too far to start backing water."

"I understand," I said.

"They've got something? Something you can't beat?"

"They've got it."

"Maybe you'd better tell me about it."

I hesitated, thinking, and finally I shook my head. "I don't think so, Mr. Walker. There's nothing you can do. Or I can do. You'd be wasting your time, and you might get Joe and yourself in a fix."

"Well, now, pshaw." He spat out the window again. "I reckon I might be a better judge of some things than you are, Mr. Ford. You—uh—aren't maybe a little distrustful, are you?"

"I think you know I'm not," I said. "I just don't want anyone else to get hurt."

"I see. Put it hypothetically, then. Just say that there are a certain set of circumstances which would have you licked—if they concerned you. Just make me up a situation that doesn't have anything to do with yours."

So I told him what they had and how they planned to use it, hypothetically. And I stumbled around a lot, because describing my situation, the evidence they had, in a hypothetical way was mighty hard to do. He got it, though, without me having to repeat a word.

"That's the whole thing?" he said. "They haven't got—they can't get, we'll say, anything in the way of actual testimony?"

"I'm pretty sure they can't," I said. "I may be wrong but I'm almost positive they couldn't get anything out of this—evidence."

"Well, then? As long as you're—"

"I know," I nodded. "They're not taking me by surprise, like they figured on. I—I mean this fellow I'm talking about—"

"Go right ahead, Mr. Ford. Just keep on using the first person. It's easier to talk that way."

"Well, I wouldn't cut loose in front of 'em. I don't think I would. But I'd do it sooner or later, with someone. It's best to have it happen now, and get it over with."

He turned his head a moment to glance at me, the big black hat flopping in the wind. "You said you didn't want anyone else to get hurt. You meant it?"

"I meant it. You can't hurt people that are already dead."

"Good enough," he said; and whether he knew what I really meant and was satisfied with it, I don't know. His ideas of right and wrong didn't jibe too close with the books.

"I sure hate to give up, though," he frowned. "Just never got in the habit of giving up, I reckon."

"You can't call it giving up," I said. "Do you see that car way back behind us? And the one up in front, the one that turned in ahead of us, a while back? Those are county cars, Mr. Walker. You're not giving up anything. It's been lost for a long time."

He glanced up into the rear-view mirror, then squinted ahead through the windshield. He spat and rubbed his hand against his pants, wiped it slowly against the soiled black cloth. "Still got quite a little ride ahead of us, Mr. Ford. About thirty miles isn't it?"

"About that. Maybe a little more."

"I wonder if you'd like to tell me about it. You don't need to, you understand, but it might be helpful. I might be able to help someone else."

"Do you think I could—that I'm able to tell you?"

"Why not?" he said. "I had a client years ago, Mr. Ford, a very able doctor. One of the most pleasant men you'd want to meet, and he had more money than he knew what to do with. But he'd performed about fifty abortions before they moved in on him, and so far as the authorities could find out every one of the abortion patients had died. He'd deliberately seen that they did die of peritonitis about a month after the operation. And he told me why—and he could've told anyone else why, when he finally faced up to the facts—he'd done it. He had a younger brother who was 'unfinished,' a prematurely born monstrosity, as the result of an attempted late-pregnancy abortion. He saw that terrible half-child die in agony for years. He never recovered from the experience—and neither did the women he aborted . . . Insane? Well, the only legal definition we have for insanity is the condition which necessitates the confinement of a person. So, since he hadn't been confined when he killed those women, I reckon he was sane. He made pretty good sense to me, anyhow."

He shifted the cud in his jaw, chewed a moment and went on. "I never had any legal schooling, Mr. Ford; picked up my law by reading in an attorney's office. All I ever had in the way of higher education was a couple years in agricultural college, and that was pretty much a plain waste of time. Crop rotation? Well, how're you going to do it when the banks only make crop loans on cotton? Soil conservation? How're you going to do terracing and draining and contour plowing when you're cropping on shares? Purebred stock? Sure. Maybe you can trade your razorbacks for Poland Chinas. . . . I just learned two things there at that college, Mr. Ford, that was ever of any use to me. One was that I couldn't do any worse than the people that were in the saddle, so maybe I'd better try pulling 'em down and riding myself. The other was a definition I got out of the agronomy books, and I reckon it was even more important than the first. It did more to revise my thinking, if I'd really done any thinking up until that time. Before that I'd seen everything in black and white, good and bad. But after I was set straight I saw that the name you put to a thing depended on where you stood and where it stood. And . . . and here's the definition, right out of the agronomy books: 'A weed is a plant out of place.' Let me repeat that. 'A weed is a plant out of place.' I find a hollyhock in my cornfield, and it's a weed. I find it in my yard, and it's a flower.

"You're in my yard, Mr. Ford."

. . . So I told him how it had been while he nodded and spat and drove, a funny pot-bellied shrimp of a guy who really had just one thing, understanding, but so much of it that you never missed anything else. He understood me better'n I understood myself.

"Yes, yes," he'd say, "you had to like people. You had to keep telling yourself you liked them. You needed to offset the deep, subconscious feelings of guilt." Or, he'd say, he'd interrupt, "and, of course, you knew you'd never leave Central City. Overprotection had made you terrified of the outside world. More important, it was part of the burden you had to carry to stay here and suffer."

He sure understood.

I reckon Billy Boy Walker's been cussed more in high places than any man in the country. But I never met a man I liked more.

I guess the way you felt about him depended on where you stood.

He stopped the car in front of my house, and I'd told him all I had to tell. But he sat there for a few minutes, spitting and sort of studying.

"Would you care to have me come in for a while, Mr. Ford?"

"I don't think it'd be smart," I said. "I got an idea it's not going to be very long, now."

He pulled an old turnip of a watch from his pocket and glanced at it. "Got a couple of hours until train time, but—well, maybe you're right. I'm sorry, Mr. Ford. I'd hoped, if I couldn't do any better, to be taking you away from here with me."

"I couldn't have gone, no matter how things were. It's like you say, I'm tied here. I'll never be free as long as I live. . . ."

25

You've got no time at all, but it seems like you've got forever. You've got nothing to do, but it seems like you've got everything.

You make coffee and smoke a few cigarettes; and the hands of the clock have gone crazy on you. They haven't moved hardly, they've hardly budged out of the place you last saw them, but they've measured off a half? two-thirds? of your life. You've got forever, but that's no time at all.

You've got forever; and somehow you can't do much with it. You've got forever; and it's a mile wide and an inch deep and full of alligators.

You go into the office and take a book or two from the shelves. You read a few lines, like your life depended on reading 'em right. But you know your life doesn't depend on anything that makes sense, and you wonder where in the hell you got the idea it did; and you begin to get sore.

You go into the laboratory and start pawing along the rows of bottles and boxes, knocking them on the floor, kicking them, stamping them. You find the bottle of one hundred percent pure nitric acid and you jerk out the rubber cork. You take it into the office and swing it along the rows of books. And the leather bindings begin to smoke and curl and wither—and it isn't good enough.

You go back into the laboratory. You come out with a gallon bottle of alcohol and the box of tall candles always kept there for emergencies. For *emergencies*.

You go upstairs, and then on up the little flight of stairs that leads to the attic. You come down from the attic and go through each of the bedrooms. You come back downstairs and go down into the basement. And when you return to the kitchen you are empty-handed. All the candles are gone, all the alcohol.

You shake the coffee pot and set it back on the stove burner. You roll another cigarette. You take a carving knife from a drawer and slide it up the sleeve of your pinkish-tan shirt with the black bow tie.

You sit down at the table with your coffee and cigarette, and you ease your elbow up and down, seeing how far you can lower your arm without dropping the knife, letting it slide down from your sleeve a time or two.

You think, *"Well how can you? How can you hurt someone that's already dead?"*

You wonder if you've done things right, so's there'll be nothing left of something that shouldn't ever have been, and you know everything has been done right. You know, because you planned this moment before eternity way back yonder someplace.

You look up at the ceiling, listening, up through the ceiling and into the sky beyond. And there isn't the least bit of doubt in your mind. That'll be the plane, all right, coming in from the east, from Fort Worth. It'll be the plane she's on.

You look up at the ceiling, grinning, and you nod and say, "Long time no see. How you been doin' anyway, huh, baby? How are you, Joyce?"

26

Just for the hell of it, I took a peek out the back door, and then I went part way into the living room and stooped down so I could look out the window. It was like I'd thought, of course. They had the house covered from every angle. Men with Winchesters. Deputies, most of 'em, with a few of the "safety inspectors" on Conway's payroll.

It would have been fun to take a real good look, to step to the door and holler howdy to 'em. But it would have been fun for them, too, and I figured they were having far too much as it was. Anyway, some of those "inspectors" were apt to be a mite trigger happy, anxious to show their boss they were on their toes, and I had a little job to do yet.

I had to get everything wrapped up to take with me.

I took one last walk through the house, and I saw that everything—the alcohol and the candles and everything—was going fine. I came back downstairs, closing all the doors behind me—*all the doors behind me*—and sat back down at the kitchen table.

The coffee pot was empty. There was just one cigarette

paper left and just enough tobacco to fill it, and, yeah—
yeah!—I was down to my last match. Things were sure
working out fine.

I puffed on the cigarette, watching the red-gray ashes
move down toward my fingers. I watched, not needing to,
knowing they'd get just so far and no further.

I heard a car pull into the driveway. I heard a couple
of its doors slam. I heard them crossing the yard and coming up the steps and across the porch. I heard the front
door open; and they came in. And the ashes had burned
out, the cigarette had gone dead.

And I laid it in my saucer and looked up.

I looked out the kitchen window, first, at the two guys
standing outside. Then I looked at them:

Conway and Hendricks, Hank Butterby and Jeff Plummer. Two or three fellows I didn't know.

They fell back, watching me, letting her move out ahead
of them. I looked at her.

Joyce Lakeland.

Her neck was in a cast that came clear up to her chin
like a collar, and she walked stiff-backed and jerky. Her
face was a white mask of gauze and tape, and nothing
much showed of it but her eyes and her lips. And she was
trying to say something—her lips were moving—but she
didn't really have a voice. She could hardly get out a whisper.

"Lou . . . I didn't . . ."

"Sure," I said. "I didn't figure you had, baby."

She kept coming toward me and I stood up, my right
arm raised like I was brushing at my hair.

I could feel my face twisting, my lips pulling back from my teeth. I knew what I must look like, but she didn't seem to mind. She wasn't scared. What did she have to be scared of?

"*. . . this, Lou. Not like this . . .*"

"Sure, you can't," I said. "Don't hardly see how you could."

"*. . . not anyway without . . .*"

"Two hearts that beat as one," I said. "T-wo—ha, ha, ha,—two—ha, ha, ha, ha, ha, ha, ha—two—J-jesus Chri—ha, ha, ha, ha, ha, ha, ha—two Jesus . . ."

And I sprang at her, I made for her just like they'd thought I would. Almost. And it was like I'd signaled, the way the smoke suddenly poured up through the floor. And the room exploded with shots and yells, and I seemed to explode with it, yelling and laughing and . . . and . . . Because they hadn't got the point. She'd got that between the ribs and the blade along with it. And they all lived happily ever after, I guess, and I guess—that's—all.

Yeah, I reckon that's all unless our kind gets another chance in the Next Place. Our kind. Us people.

All of us that started the game with a crooked cue, that wanted so much and got so little, that meant so good and did so bad. All us folks. Me and Joyce Lakeland, and Johnnie Pappas and Bob Maples and big ol' Elmer Conway and little ol' Amy Stanton. All of us.

All of us.

About the Author

James Meyers Thompson was born in Anadarko, Oklahoma, in 1906. He began writing fiction at a very young age, selling his first story to *True Detective* when he was only fourteen. In all, Jim Thompson wrote twenty-nine novels and two screenplays (for the Stanley Kubrick films *The Killing* and *Paths of Glory*). Films based on his novels include: *Coup de Torchon (Pop. 1280)*, *Serie Noire (A Hell of a Woman)*, *The Getaway*, *The Killer Inside Me*, *The Grifters*, and *After Dark, My Sweet*. A biography of Jim Thompson will be published by Knopf.